The Notebooks of Malte Laurids Brigge

Originally published in German as *Die Aufzeichnungen des Malte Laurids Brigge* by Insel Verlag, 1910

Library of Congress Cataloging-in-Publication Data

Rilke, Rainer Maria, 1875-1926.
[Aufzeichnungen des Malte Laurids Brigge. English]
The notebooks of Malte Laurids Brigge / Rainer Maria Rilke ;
translation by Burton Pike. -- 1st Dalkey Archive ed.
    p. cm.
ISBN 978-1-56478-497-1 (pbk. : alk. paper)
I. Pike, Burton. II. Title.
PT2635.I65A813 2009
833'.912--dc22

2008016100

Partially funded by a grant from the Illinois Arts Council, a state agency, and by the University of Illinois at Urbana-Champaign

Cover art by Nicholas Motte / design by Danielle Dutton

www.dalkeyarchive.com

The Notebooks of Malte Laurids Brigge
by Rainer Maria Rilke

Translated from the German by Burton Pike

Dalkey Archive Press ⬚ Champaign and London

Introduction

The Notebooks of Malte Laurids Brigge was published in 1910. Rilke had been working on it since 1904. This was the period of his most intense struggle to reinvent himself as a poet, the period that saw the publication of his *New Poems* (1906, 1907) and other poems that mark this ongoing effort. From a technical point of view, writing this novel gave Rilke endless trouble. He experimented with it for quite some time before settling on a final technique and narrative. The *Notebooks* is among the first Modernist novels—those that rejected nineteenth-century conventions of plot and character and attempted to find new forms for the novel in a radically changing European culture. In this endeavor *The Notebooks of Malte Laurids Brigge* ("Aufzeichnungen" can also be translated as "sketchbooks") has arguably been among the most influential works of modern fiction.

This novel points forward to the *Duino Elegies* and *Sonnets to Orpheus*, but it is also important to see it from the outside, to ask with what other works of literature it might be compared. Malte, at twenty-eight, desperately wants to be a poet. He is an artist-figure strongly driven by his will to transform reality into a new kind of art, but he lacks the synthesizing power to succeed. His author makes him try, but fail. The reader of German literature will be reminded of two artist figures in the same predicament, Werther in Goethe's *The Sorrows of Young Werther*, and Tonio Kröger in Thomas Mann's novella *Tonio Kröger*. Like Werther and Tonio, Malte is a weaker artist standing in for the strong artist who is actually writing the book and who succeeds in creating art where the surrogate character fails. All three works contain strong autobiographical elements: they are, among other things, records of difficult personal as well as technical problems that their authors had to work through, and of inner problems they felt they had to overcome. (Malte's misery as an impoverished young foreigner in Paris was Rilke's own.)

The poetic crisis Rilke went through shortly after the turn of the twentieth century was a common one for his generation of writers, the generation after Nietzsche, and must be seen in that context. It was Nietzsche who largely codified the revolution in thought and values that characterized the later nineteenth century in Europe. Nietzsche's counterparts in the natural sciences, psychology, and philosophy—Mach, Einstein, William James, Bergson, and Freud, among many others—were ushering in a new basis for thought based on experimental thinking and the rejection of received values. Uncertainty replaced determinism as the fundamental principle, and the notion of a coherent self was radically stripped of its central, fixed identity.

Rilke, born in 1875, had been a facile and voluble poet when he was young, writing in what was by then worn-out shreds of the imagery of romanticism: easy sentimentality, languishing figures in the moonlight, a dim chivalric past. But Rilke, ambitious and extremely intelligent, saw after a while that that kind of literature was over, along with the tradition it had been part of. He was alert to the fresh breeze blowing through European culture around and after 1900. Very much like Thomas Mann, Kafka, Musil, Hofmannsthal, Proust, Ezra Pound, Virginia Woolf, T. S. Eliot, Mahler, Schoenberg, Picasso, and so many others, Rilke faced in two directions, toward a tradition whose conventions had faded away and toward the challenge of creating a new kind of art for a new European culture. Like other writers of the time, he was following Pound's dictum to "make it new," but like them Rilke was doing so out of the remnants of the past. (His extensive use of documentary sources in this novel is explored in the Note at the end of this volume.) These remnants function for Malte much as do the chain of unattributed quotations for the anonymous narrator of T. S. Eliot's *The Waste Land*: "These fragments I have shored against my ruins."

Perhaps more than most of these other writers, artists, and composers, Rilke in his poetry and prose records a deep sense of loss, of mourning a vanished world. There is in *The Notebooks* a profound split between this sense of loss and Rilke's—and Malte's—dogged attempts to reconceptualize art in a way that would recover the past in a newly dislocated and fragmented world. Clear as Malte is about the new task he feels called upon to undertake, one often has the impression that he has been expelled into the twentieth century rather than embracing it. However, the radically experimental language of the novel, breathtaking in its boldness and beauty, is another matter. Malte, his emotions tied to the old order, regards the new one with a kind of anguish, but at the same time throws himself wholeheartedly into the task of transformation. Rilke's self-imposed task was to find how, in new terms, he could accomplish what Valéry called the sovereign act of the artist, "the passage from the arbitrary to the necessary."

For Rilke this was a particularly difficult task, since he combined a belief in a supra-reality revealed in things with an exceptionally concrete poetic vision. He actively kept up with the world of art and ideas, read very widely, and was personally acquainted with important artists and writers of his day. What he strove to achieve in his art can be called a state of "day-bright mysticism," in the phrase of his contemporary and admirer Robert Musil.

The problem Rilke faced was how to register the transitory and inert details of a demystified world and so transform them inwardly that they could achieve the objective permanence of art in a time when art had lost all guiding traditions and forms. This called for a new concept of seeing. The thing that is seen, the object to be transformed, can be anything: a blind hawker of newspapers, a cauliflower peddler, also blind. It can be anything in Malte's childhood or from the remote past. He admires Baudelaire's grisly poem "A Carcass" (*Une Charogne*) because it transforms the most repulsive subject imaginable, the decaying corpse of a dead woman, into the art of poetry. It is something that shocks and will continue to shock readers, who would never "see" the rotting corpse if Baudelaire had not "seen" it as a poem. Malte admires Ibsen, Beethoven, and the actress Eleonora Duse for their driving will to make things new, to make the invisible world of the past visible again through an enduring world of art. But theirs is a challenge Malte is not equal to. He can only make attempt after attempt. Thus it is no surprise that Rilke's novel ends in the episode of the Prodigal Son with a "not yet." Refusing the world's terms, Malte is unable to rejoin the world on his own, and he is unable to transform the real into art. Like so many other Modernist writers, Rilke could not end his novel in a way commensurate with its experimental, open form. It is the record of a process that, for its author, was in any case not concluded.

Rilke laid out Malte's problem on three complex levels: first, Malte's reality as he lives it in the present and tries to make art out of it; second, his recalled childhood, the reality he personally remembers; and third, the reality that Malte ingests from great artists, medieval tapestries, foreign places, stories, and long-forgotten historical figures and battles. Malte fails to make art out of his lived present reality, which is, on the whole, harshly described. His childhood memories are more evocative and on the way to becoming stories, but he seems to be still too invested in them personally to create a necessary distance. The old historical figures and events have too much distance, evoking as they do a world that is totally strange to us and without connection to the modern world for which Malte is restoring them to visibility. These levels are all brought to a focus in Malte's consciousness as he struggles to embed these disparate fragments into an art of enduring permanence.

The third level, that of the medieval stories and remote figures of the past, is the most problematic for the reader. Rilke felt strongly that historical names and references in the text should not be identified, because for him their importance lay not in their reference to history but in the way they impinge on and become part of Malte's consciousness. It doesn't matter *who* these figures were beyond what is recorded about them in the novel; Malte's *patterning* of them is clear enough, and is made explicit in his evocation of the Unicorn tapestries. Rilke's ingenious interweaving of the three levels shows how all three could be evoked in art, the art of his novel. It is an art that, for both Malte and Rilke is obsessively devoted to being accurate to reality in both past and present. (This obsession, with a sample of Rilke's sources, is discussed in the Note at the end.)

For the Rilke of the *Notebooks*, and Malte in his present time, transformation was to be achieved through scrupulous observation of the actual raw data of history, life, and sensory experience as these impinge directly on consciousness. This was what a new way of seeing involved. What the English philosopher T. E. Hulme wrote in his essay "Romanticism and Classicism" in 1913 neatly characterizes Rilke's stance and the stance Malte is struggling to achieve:

> There are . . . two things to distinguish, first the particular faculty of mind to see things as they really are, and apart from the conventional ways in which you have been trained to see them. . . . Second, the concentrated state of mind, the grip over oneself which is necessary in the actual expression of what one sees. To prevent one falling into the conventional curves of ingrained technique, to hold on through infinite detail and trouble to the exact curve you want.

The central problem for Rilke and other writers and artists of the time was how to make high art out of a world and a notion of self that had been totally revolutionized. Paul Valéry, a kindred spirit with whom Rilke was on friendly terms, wrote how traditional subject matter and styles had gone out of fashion in painting: "Landscape invades the walls abandoned by Greeks, Turks, nobles, and cupids. Landscape ruins the notion of the *subject*, and in the space of a few years has reduced the whole intellectual part of art to debates on *material* and the color of shadows. The brain has become pure retina."[1] In Rilke's *New Poems*, written while he was working on *The Notebooks*, he experimented with penetrating beyond retinal surfaces to a new way of seeing and representing. In 1908 he wrote an eloquent *Requiem* for Count Kalckreuth, a young poet who had committed

---

1   Valéry's emphasis. My translation.

suicide. This poem addresses what was also Malte's central concern: in times of such radical change, how is one to be a poet? ("The great words from those times / when happening was still visible are not for us" we read in the *Requiem*.)

The radical form of Rilke's only novel is a challenging departure. How can something called "notebooks" or "sketchbooks" be a novel? And indeed this novel is not a coherent narrative but a series of disconnected, random scenes, each one poignant and beautifully realized. There are various characters and many vivid incidents but no plot, and the Malte who is noting things down takes everything in but has only a vague identity. His self is not capable of binding everything together into a synthesis. Malte is no longer a character, but an energy field crisscrossed and overrun by sensations and memories. (Rilke here seems indebted to the sociologist Georg Simmel, whose seminal essay "The Metropolis and Mental Life" appeared in 1903. Rilke read Simmel and knew him socially in Berlin.) Driven by will, Malte constantly hovers in uncertainty while groping for certainty. He frequently refers to himself not with the first person pronoun, "I," but with the indefinite pronoun "one" (*man*) instead.

Malte is, deliberately, hard for the reader to grasp. Rilke made him that way for a purpose: the author's focus is not on who Malte is, but on how he experiences things in his quest for a new basis for art. That is why these are "notebooks" rather than "diaries." Rilke avoids using a stream-of-consciousness technique because that would be a purely internal process, completely contained within the character's consciousness. This is not an Existentialist novel like one of its later imitations, Sartre's *Nausea*. Both Rilke and Malte try again and again to objectify the world rather than their own consciousnesses. "No, no, one can imagine nothing in the world, not the least thing," Malte writes. "Everything is composed of so many isolated details that are not to be foreseen. In one's imagining one passes over them and hasty as one is doesn't notice that they are missing. But realities are slow and indescribably detailed."

Rilke deeply admired Cézanne as a pioneer of a new way of forging humble observed details into an artistic vision, and one thinks of Cubist and Expressionist painters as engaged in the same endeavor.

"Seeing" is central to understanding the *Notebooks*. "I am learning to see," Malte says at the beginning, and "I am afraid." The solitary artist cast loose in the world in the shadow of death will attempt to revitalize art by reconceptualizing seeing. It is Malte's obsession with death that makes this process the urgent task of his life.

Rilke charts a radical departure from commonsense notions of seeing. It is a scrupulous registering of the data of what is seen by the artist-observer's mind, with the idea, or hope, that much later it might suddenly coalesce into a work of art. This purposive seeing involves great patience, involves a long act of *waiting*. The poet has the will, but does not control this process. (Rilke seems to have developed this notion from Cézanne and Rodin.) Malte writes:

> But alas, with poems one accomplishes so little when one writes them early. One should hold off and gather sense and sweetness a whole life long, a long life if possible, and then, right at the end, one could write perhaps ten lines that are good. For poems are not, as people think, feelings (those one has early enough)—they are experiences. For the sake of a line of poetry one must see many cities, people, and things, one must know animals, must feel how the birds fly, and know the gestures with which small flowers open in the morning . . . But it is still not enough to have memories. One must be able to forget them, if they are many, and have the great patience to wait for them to come again. For it

is not the memories themselves. Only when they become blood in us, glance and gesture, nameless and no longer to be distinguished from ourselves, only then can it happen that in a very rare hour the first word of a line arises in their midst and strides out of them.

And in the *Requiem* for Count Kalckreuth Rilke states the goal, the result of this patient waiting: for fate "to enter the line of poetry and not come out again." The patience necessary to turn will and scrupulous observation into art is something Malte feels deeply; one might almost call it the principle that paralyzes him. For Malte the price of this will to wait and to observe is living in a state of complete inner and outer isolation. To keep himself perpetually in a state of seeing and waiting involves willing the sacrifice of separation from family, friends, and society. Hence the inability of the Prodigal Son at the end of the novel to accept the love of the family to which he has returned. They can see him only in the framework of their own lives, not as he is in his own. The waiting and separation from others involves intense suffering for Malte, even a nervous breakdown, but what drives him and this novel, as its title indicates, is not despair at existence but an intense dedication to art as a high calling for which these are the "sketches." The waiting is a necessary act of will. Hence Malte's fascination, amounting to an obsession, with saints, artists, outcasts, and historical figures whose wills were single-mindedly dedicated to their calling.

For Malte, seeing involves more than the optical-visual sense. He sees by sound—the electric tram rushing through Malte's room; by hearing—the Danish singer in Venice; memories, which Malte reconstitutes as visual scenes, those of his childhood, for instance. Or through empathy—the man in the street with the nervous disorder, the dying man in the small restaurant. Or through reading:

bringing documents from the past to life before the reader's eyes by re-inscribing them. Malte's grandfather, Count Brahe, is in this sense a central figure in this novel. For Count Brahe, there is no past or future: things that have happened or will happen exist for him as present and visible events, and this is true for Malte's memories and evocations as well. It is not the temporal categories of past, present, and future that matter, but a spatial notion, visible/invisible. Re-creating, re-inscribing this past is a way of making the invisible visible again, for the writer and the reader. The walking ghost of Christine Brahe is one example of this visualized invisibility; others are Malte's revivifying evocation of the Unicorn tapestries or his bringing to life Froissart's medieval *Chronicles*. All the episodes Malte records in his notebooks are haunting and intense, filled with the energy of present, visualized happening. Malte turns all these scenes into visible "seeing" as he re-creates them and writes them down. "Suddenly one has the right eyes" Rilke wrote to his wife on October 10, 1907, after seeing a Cézanne exhibition in Paris. But Malte can not get beyond the raw material, can not find a coherent framework within which to order his perceived and recalled bits and pieces. ("But now, please, a narrator, a narrator!" he pleads in frustration at one point.)

That everything Malte "sees" is seen in order to internalize it explains why famous historical artist-figures are clearly presented but not identified by name. What Malte responds to in them is their ability to visualize what was invisible to others, a force that led them steadily and surely, against public incomprehension and resistance, to revolutionize their respective arts, something Malte can not achieve and Rilke is trying to. The same applies to the famous women lovers of history, who are named but not identified; their driving will is love, something else that Malte cannot achieve for himself, and that is felt to be an impediment to his breaking through as an artist. Identifying these figures is not the point; it is what they represent for Malte, not who they are, that matters. Ibsen himself bears witness to this single-minded will that Malte responds to in him, as well as in Beethoven and Eleanora Duse. In a letter to the Danish critic Georg Brandes in 1883 Ibsen wrote:

> An intellectual pioneer can never gather a majority about him. In ten years the majority may have reached that standpoint which Dr. Stockmann [in *An Enemy of the People*] had reached when the people held their meeting. But during those ten years the Doctor has not remained stationary; he still stands at least ten years ahead of the others. The majority, the masses, the mob, will never catch him up; he can never rally them behind him. I myself feel a similarly unrelenting compulsion to keep pressing forward. A crowd now stands where I stood when I wrote my earlier books. But I myself am there no longer. I am somewhere else—far ahead of them—or so I hope.[2]

Rilke's point was that Malte's retelling of these stories makes them present again, moments recaptured from the lost, dead past and so once again made visible by the artist in a new context. The reader is meant to "see" these moments as Malte does and in reference to him, not as historical references. Rilke was quite explicit about this. Toward the end of his life, on November 10, 1925, he wrote to his Polish translator, Witold von Hulewicz:

> In Malte there can be no talk of making the numerous evo-

---

2 Quoted in Michael Meyer, "Introduction" to *Henrik Ibsen: The Wild Duck, Hedda Gabler*, trans. Michael Meyer (New York: W. W. Norton, 1977 <1961>), p. 4.

cations more precise and isolating them. The reader is to communicate not with their historical or imaginary reality, but through them with Malte's experience. . . . [Like Ibsen, who] searched for a demonstration in the visible of the event that had become invisible within us, the young M. L. Brigge also desires to make graspable through phenomena and pictures the life that is continually withdrawing into the invisible. . . . And all these things, wherever he might have experienced them, have for him the same worth, the same enduring quality and presentness. . . . [The figures] are not historical figures or forms from [Malte's] own past, but *words of his desperate need*, that is why from time to time a name is mentioned without being further explained . . . (Rilke's emphasis).

Malte aims for a unity he cannot reach, but his honesty keeps him from faking it, and the honesty of his attempts is one of the signal accomplishments of Rilke's novel. Malte writes of the dying Danish poet Felix Arvers that "he was a poet and hated the approximate." In the *Requiem* for Count Kalckreuth as well, Rilke attacks poets who think that to write poetry is to parade their feelings:

> . . . Like sick people
> they use language full of self-pity
> to describe where they are hurting,
> instead of stubbornly transforming themselves into the
> words
> as the stonemason of a cathedral
> doggedly translates himself into the composure of the
> stone.

Proust wrote in *Against Saint-Beuve* that "the finest books are written in a kind of foreign language," and this is certainly true of the *Notebooks*. Its rigorously experimental language is intense, compressed, and vividly metaphorical. The attempt to find the right kind of language, of necessity a "foreign" one in Proust's sense, meant in Rilke's case creating a new language for a new kind of novel. Rilke's language is quite different from that of his contemporaries and from earlier German prose styles; it is reminiscent of Baudelaire's prose poems and poetry. The novel's style is closer to poetry than to prose; so many of the beautifully etched episodes are indelible in their precise melding of word, metaphor, and visualizations of people, places, and things. This language is conspicuously controlled; its strong grip inexorably pulls the reader into Malte's obsessions. The reader, dislocated as observer, is made to "see" things through Malte's eyes and mind rather than his own.

Rilke's prose in this novel is arresting, haunting, and beautiful, but it is not smooth. His style is explicit, direct, almost laconic, and it has an edge. I have tried to retain these qualities in my translation. It would be a mistake to translate his German into a smoothed-over literary English. That would be to overemphasize the existential element of Malte's tribulations, and to obscure the radically experimental and daring nature of Rilke's prose. The footnotes in the text, which are mine unless otherwise indicated, provide translations and necessary information.

For my understanding of *The Notebooks* I am indebted to the rich trove of fine Rilke scholarship in a number of languages to which a great many people have contributed over the years. I am most grateful to Peter Constantine for his encouragement and support, and to Hanne-Lore Boddin and Helene Sakellion for their help with knotty problems of Rilke's language.

Burton Pike, 2007

The Notebooks of Malte Laurids Brigge

Book One

September 11, rue Toullier

So, this is where people come in order to live, I would have rather thought: to die. I have been out. I have seen: hospitals. I saw a man who tottered and collapsed. People gathered around him, that spared me the rest. I saw a pregnant woman. She was pushing herself with difficulty along a high warm wall, which she sometimes reached out to touch as if to convince herself that it was still there. Yes, it was still there. And behind it? I looked on my map: *Maison d'Accouchement.* Good. They will deliver her—they can do that. Further on, rue Saint-Jacques, a big building with a dome. The map indicated *Val-de-Grâce, Hôpital militaire.* I didn't really need to know that, but it does no harm. The street began to smell from all sides. It smelled, as far as one could distinguish, of iodoform, of the grease of pommes frites, of fear. All cities smell in summer. Then I saw a curiously cataract-blinded building, it wasn't to be found on the map, but over the door it said, fairly legibly: *Asyle de nuit*.[1] Beside the entrance were the prices. I read them. It was not expensive.

And what else? A child in a standing baby carriage. The child was fat, greenish, and had a prominent sore on its forehead. The sore was obviously healing and did not hurt. The child was sleeping, its mouth open, breathing iodoform, pommes frites, fear. That's how it was. The main thing was that one was alive. That was the main thing.

That I can't give up sleeping with the window open. Electric trolleys race ringing through my room. Automobiles rush over me. A door slams shut. Somewhere a pane of glass shatters, I hear the big fragments laugh, the small splinters titter. Then, suddenly, a muffled, confined noise from the other side, within the building. Someone is climbing the stairs. Coming, incessantly coming. Is here, is here a long time, passes by. And the street again. A girl screams: *Ah tais-toi, je ne veux plus.*[2] The trolley comes running up all excited, runs on over it, over everything. Someone calls out. People are running, overtake each other. A dog barks. What a relief: a dog. Toward morning even a cock crows, and that is an indescribable blessing. Then I suddenly fall asleep.

Those are the noises. But there is something here that is even more terrible: the silence. I think that sometimes there is such a moment of extreme tension at great fires: the waterhoses fall away, the firemen are no longer climbing, no one moves. Soundlessly a black pediment up above pushes forward, and a high wall behind which

---

1   Maison d'Accouchement: Lying-in-Hospital. Asyle de nuit: flophouse.

2   Oh shut up, I've had enough.

the fire flares up starts to lean out, soundlessly. Everyone stands and waits with hunched shoulders, faces furrowed above the eyes, waiting for the horrible crash. That's what the silence here is like.

I am learning to see. I don't know why, everything penetrates me more deeply, and doesn't stop at the place where it always used to end. There is a place in me I knew nothing about. Everything goes there now. I don't know what goes on there.

Today I wrote a letter, it made me realize that I have only been here for three weeks. Three weeks someplace else, in the country for example, could be like a day, here it is years. I don't intend to write any more letters. Why should I tell someone that I am changing? If I change, I am no longer the person I was, and if I am something different than before it is clear that I have no acquaintances. And it is impossible for me to write to strangers, to people who do not know me.

Have I said it already? I am learning to see. Yes, I'm beginning. It is still going badly. But I want to make use of my time.

For instance, I never realized how many faces there are. There are lots of people but still more faces, for everyone has several. There are people who wear a face for years, of course it wears out, gets dirty, cracks in the folds, stretches like a glove one has worn on a journey. Those are thrifty, simple people: they don't change it, they don't even have it cleaned. It's good enough, they maintain, and who can convince them otherwise? The question does arise, since they have several faces, what do they do with the others? They keep them in reserve. Their children will get to wear them. But it also happens that their dogs wear them when they go out. And why not? Face is face.

Other people put on their faces with uncanny rapidity, one after the other, and wear them all out. At first it seems to them as if they would have them forever, but they are barely forty and this one is already the last. That of course has its tragic side. They are not used to taking care of faces, they run through their last one in a week, there are holes in it, in many places it is as thin as paper, and then slowly what's underneath emerges, the not-face, and they walk around with that.

But the woman, the woman: she had fallen completely into herself, forward into her hands. It was on the corner of the rue Nôtre-Dame-des-Champs. As soon as I saw her I began to walk softly. When poor people are thinking of something one should not disturb them. Perhaps it will occur to them.

The street was too empty, its emptiness got bored and pulled my foot out from under and flipped it back and forth, this way and that, like a wooden shoe. The woman took fright and raised herself up out of herself, too quickly, too violently, so that her face remained in her two hands. I could see it laying there, its hollow form. It cost me an indescribable effort to stay with those hands and not to look at what had torn itself out of them. I dreaded seeing a face from the inside, but I was even more afraid of the exposed, flayed head without a face.

I am afraid. Against fear, once one has it, one must do something. It would be truly hateful to get sick here, and if it should occur to anyone to hustle me off to the Hôtel-Dieu,[3] I would certainly die there. This Hôtel is a pleasant Hôtel, fantastically busy. One can hardly contemplate the façade of the Cathedral of Paris without the

---

3   Hôtel-Dieu: The large old central hospital of Paris.

danger of being run over by one of the many vehicles rushing toward its entrance across the open square as fast as they can. They are small omnibuses continuously sounding their bells, and even the Duke of Sagan would have to stop his coach if some small dying person had got it into his head to try to get straight into God's Hotel. Dying people are pigheaded, and all Paris comes to a halt when Madame Legrand, dealer in second-hand goods from the rue des Martyrs, is driven to a particular square of the Cité. It is to be noted that these small fiendish vehicles have uncommonly stimulating milk-glass windows behind which one can conjure up the most splendid agonies; it only takes the imagination of a concierge. If one has more imagination and casts it in other directions, the possibilities are absolutely limitless. But I have often seen open carriages arriving, taxis with their tops down, driving for the usual fare: two francs for the hour of death.

This excellent Hôtel is quite old, people were already dying in it in several beds in King Chlodwig's time. Now there is dying in 559 beds. Factory-style, of course. With such enormous production the individual death is not carried out so well, but that's not what matters either. It's a question of numbers. Who today will pay something for a death that has been well worked out? No one. Even the rich, who could afford to die in great detail, are beginning to get careless and indifferent: the desire to have a death of one's own is becoming ever rarer. In a short while it will be just as rare as a life of one's own. God, everything is presented ready-made. One comes along, one finds a life all prepared, one only has to put it on. One wants to leave or is forced to; no strain: *Voilà votre mort, monsieur.*[4] One dies as one happens to; one dies the death that belongs to the disease one has (for since all diseases are known, one also knows that their various fatal conclusions belong to the diseases and not to the person, and the ill person has, so to speak, nothing to do).

In the sanatoriums, where people die so gladly and are so grateful to the doctors and nurses, one dies one of the deaths employed by the institution; that is looked upon with approval. But if one dies at home, it is a matter of course to choose the polite death of better circles, with which, so to speak, the first-class burial already begins, with its whole sequence of simply beautiful rituals. The poor stand before such a house and look their fill. *Their* death is of course banal, without any fuss. They are happy if they find one that more or less fits. It's all right if it's too big: one always still grows a little. Only if death doesn't come on through the chest, or strangles, then it has its difficulty.

When I think of home, where no one is any longer, I believe that earlier it must have been different. Earlier one knew (or perhaps surmised) that one had death *within* oneself, like fruit the seed. Children had a small death in themselves and grownups a big one. Women had it in their wombs and men in their chests. One *had* it, and that gave one a special dignity and a quiet pride.

One saw in my grandfather, old Chamberlain Brigge, that he bore a death within himself. And what a death it was: two months long, and so loud it could be heard even as far as the outlying buildings.

---

4   Here is your death, sir.

The long, old main house was too small for this death, it seemed as if wings would need to be added to it, for the chamberlain's body became larger and larger, and he was continually demanding to be carried from one room to the next, and fell into a terrible rage when the day was not yet done and there were no longer any rooms in which he had not already lain. Then the whole procession of servants, maids, and dogs, which he always had around him, came up the stairs and, the house steward at their head, into the room where his blessèd mother had died, the room that had been preserved exactly as she had left it twenty-three years before and that otherwise no one had ever been allowed to enter. Now the whole pack burst in. The draperies were drawn back, and the robust light of a summer afternoon investigated all the shy, startled objects and turned around awkwardly in the ripped-open mirrors. And the people did the same. There were maids who were so curious they didn't know where their hands had got to, young servants who gaped at everything, and older ones who went around and sought to remember what they had been told about this locked room in which they now happily found themselves.

But above all, being in a room where all the objects smelled seemed uncommonly exciting for the dogs. The big, lean Russian greyhounds ran busily back and forth behind the armchairs, criss-crossing the room with a rocking motion in a long dance-step, raised themselves up like dogs in a coat of arms, their thin paws supported on the white and gold window sill, and stared into the courtyard left and right with pointed, tensed faces and drawn-back foreheads. Small, glove-yellow dachshunds sat in the wide, plumped-up silk armchairs by the window, with faces as if everything was as it should be, and a wiry-haired, sullen-looking pointer rubbed his back on the edge of a gold-legged table on whose painted top the Sèvres cups trembled.

Yes, for these absent-minded things heavy with sleep it was a terrible time. It happened that rose petals tumbled out of books some hasty hand had awkwardly opened and were crushed underfoot; small, fragile objects were picked up and, after they immediately broke, quickly set down again; many damaged things were hidden behind curtains or even thrown behind the golden weave of the fireplace screen. And from time to time something fell down, fell muffled on the carpet, fell brightly on the hard parquet, but in either case it broke, burst sharply or broke open almost soundlessly, for cosseted as they were, these objects could not withstand any kind of fall.

And if it had occurred to anyone to ask what was the cause of everything that had called down the fullness of all this destruction on this anxiously guarded room—there would have been only *one* answer: death.

The death of the chamberlain Christoph Detlev Brigge at Ulsgaard. For, swelling out of his dark blue uniform, he lay in the middle of the floor and did not stir. In his large, strange face, no longer familiar to anyone, his eyes had fallen shut: he did not see what was happening. At first they had attempted to lay him on the bed, but he had put up a struggle, for he hated beds ever since those first nights in which his illness had grown. And then the bed up there turned out to be too small, so there was nothing else to do but lay him on the carpet as he was; for he had not wanted to go downstairs.

So there he lay, and one might think that he had died. As the light slowly began to fade the dogs had withdrawn through the crack of the door, one after another, only the wire-haired pointer with the sullen face sat by his master, and one of his broad, shaggy front paws lay on Christoph Detlev's large gray hand. Most of the servants too were standing outside in the white corridor, which was brighter than the room; but those who had remained inside sometimes stole a glance at the big, darkening heap in the middle, wishing that it were nothing more than a large suit covering some ruined thing.

But it was still something. It was a voice, the voice that seven weeks before no one had recognized: for it was not the voice of the chamberlain. It was not Christoph Detlev to whom this voice belonged, it was Christoph Detlev's death.

Christoph Detlev's death had now been living for many, many days at Ulsgaard, and spoke with everyone and demanded. Demanded to be carried around, demanded the blue room, demanded the small salon, demanded the large hall. Demanded the dogs, demanded that people laugh, speak, play, and be silent, and all at the same time. Demanded to see friends, women, and those who had died, and demanded himself to die: demanded. Demanded and screamed.

For when night had come and those of the exhausted servants who were not keeping watch tried to get to sleep, then Christoph Detlev's death screamed, screamed and moaned, roared so long and so incessantly that the dogs, who at first howled along, fell silent and did not dare lie down but, standing on their long, slender, quivering legs, were afraid. And when those in the village heard him roaring through the far, silver, Danish summer night, they got up as for a thunderstorm, dressed, and sat around the lamp without saying a word until it was over. And the women who were near to giving birth were put in the most remote rooms and the most shielded bedcupboards; but they heard it, heard it as if it were in their own bodies, and they pleaded to get up too and came, broad and pale, and sat down among the others with their blurred faces. And the cows that were calving at this time were helpless and withdrawn, and the dead fruit was torn out of the body with all the entrails when it wouldn't come. And everyone performed their daily tasks badly and forgot to bring in the hay, because during the day they feared for the night and because they were so exhausted from being up so much and from getting up frightened that they could not think of anything. And when on Sundays they went into the peaceful white church, they prayed that Ulsgaard should no longer have a master, for this was a dreadful master. And what they were all thinking and praying the pastor said out loud from the chancel, for he too no longer had any nights and could not understand God. And the bell said it, which had acquired a fearsome rival that tolled the entire night and with which the bell could not compete, even when it began ringing out from all its metal. Yes, everyone said it, and among the young people was one who had dreamed that he had gone to the castle and beat the master to death with a manure fork, and people were so angry, so exhausted, so irritated, that they all listened as he related his dream, and without even knowing it looked at him to see if he were up to such a deed. That is how one felt and spoke in the whole region, in which a few weeks before the chamberlain had been loved and pitied. But even though people spoke this way, nothing changed. Christoph Detlev's death that lived at Ulsgaard was not to be hurried. It had come for ten weeks, and for ten weeks it remained. And during this time it was more the master than Christoph Detlev had ever been, it was like a king whom one calls the Terrible, later and always.

It was not the death of any dropsy sufferer, it was the angry, princely death that the chamberlain had carried within himself his whole life long and had nourished out of himself. All the excess of pride, will, and energy of mastery that he himself had not been able to use up even in his calm days had gone into his death, which now sat at Ulsgaard and squandered it.

How Chamberlain Brigge would have looked at him who would have desired of him that he should die another death than this. He died his difficult death.

And when I think of the others I have seen or whom I have heard about: it is always the same. They all had their own death. These men who bore it within their armor, inside, like a prisoner, these women who became very old and small and then passed over in an enormous bed, as on a stage, before the entire family, the servants, and the dogs, grandly and discreetly. The children, even quite little ones, did not have some child's death or other, but pulled themselves together and died what they already were and what they would have become.

And what kind of melancholy beauty did it give women when they were pregnant and standing, and in their big bodies, on which their narrow hands involuntarily rested, were *two* fruits: a child and a death. Did not the concentrated, almost nourishing smile in their completely emptied-out faces come from their sometimes thinking that both were growing?

I have done something against the fear. I have sat up all night and written, and now I am as worn out as after a long walk across the fields of Ulsgaard. It is hard to think that all that is no more, that strangers live in the long, old main house. It may be that in the white room up in the gable the maids now sleep, sleep their heavy, damp sleep from evening to morning.

And one has no one and nothing and roams about in the world with a suitcase and a box of books and really without curiosity. What sort of life is that, really: without a house, without inherited things, without dogs. If one at least had one's memories. But who has them? If childhood is present, it is as if buried. Perhaps one must be old to be able to get hold of all that. I think to myself it is good to be old.

Today was a beautiful fall morning. I walked through the Tuileries. Everything toward the east, into the sun, was blinding. The things shone upon were covered by fog as by a light gray curtain. Gray in gray, the statues sunned themselves in the not yet unveiled garden. Single flowers stood up in the long beds and said "red" in a startled voice. Then a thin, very tall man came around the corner, from the Champs-Elysées; he was carrying a crutch, but no longer shoved under his shoulder: he was holding it out in front of him, casually, and from time to time he stamped it down firmly and loudly, like a herald's staff. He could not suppress a smile of joy, and smiled, past everything, to the sun, the trees. His step was timid like a child's but exceptionally light, full of the memory of earlier walking.

All the things such a little moon can do. There are days when around one everything is lit, delicate, hardly outlined in the bright air, and yet clear. Even the closest things have tones of distance, are removed and only sketched, not handed to one; and whatever has connection to distance: the river, the bridges, the long streets, and the squares that squander themselves, all this the distance has gathered behind itself, is painted on it as if on silk. It is impossible to say what a pale green vehicle on the Pont Neuf can be in this light, or some kind of red that the eye cannot retain, or even a poster on the firewall of a pearl-gray group of houses. Everything is simplified, reduced to a few straight, bright planes like the face in a Manet portrait. And nothing is insignificant or superfluous. The booksellers on the quai are opening their stands, and the fresh or faded yellow of the books, the violet brown of the volumes, the stronger green of a folder: everything is in place, is valid, partaking, and forms a completeness in which nothing is lacking.

On the street below there is the following grouping: a small hand-cart, pushed by a woman; on top, in front, a hurdy-gurdy, lengthwise. Diagonally behind it a child's crib in which a very small child stands on firm legs, happy in its bonnet and refusing to stay sitting down. From time to time the woman cranks the hurdy-gurdy. The very small child then immediately gets up again, stamping in its crib, and a little girl in a green Sunday dress dances and beats a tambourine up toward the windows.

I think I should begin to work on something, now that I am learning to see. I am twenty-eight, and just about nothing has happened. Let's summarize: I have written a study of Carpaccio, which is bad, a drama called *Marriage* that tries to prove something false by ambiguous means, and poems. But alas, with poems one accomplishes so little when one writes them early. One should hold off and gather sense and sweetness a whole life long, a long life if possible, and then, right at the end, one could perhaps write ten lines that are good. For poems are not, as people think, feelings (those one has early enough—they are experiences. For the sake of a line of poetry one must see many cities, people, and things, one must know animals, must feel how the birds fly, and know the gestures with which small flowers open in the morning. One must be able to think back to paths in unknown regions, to unexpected meetings and to partings one long saw coming; to childhood days that are still not understood, to parents one had to hurt when they brought one a joy and one did not understand it (it was a joy to someone else); to childhood illnesses that set in so strangely with so many profound and heavy transformations, to days in quiet, muted rooms and to mornings by the sea, the sea altogether, to nights travelling that rushed up and away and flew with all the stars; and if one can think of all that, it is still not enough. One must have memories of many nights of love, none of which resembled another, of screams in the delivery room and of easy, pale, sleeping women delivered, who are closing themselves. But one must also have been with the dying, have sat by the dead in the room with the open window and the spasmodic noises. But it is still not enough to have memories. One must be able to forget them, if they are many, and have the great patience to wait for them to come again. For it is not the memories themselves. Only when they become blood in us, glance and gesture, nameless and no longer to be distinguished from ourselves, only then can it happen that in a very rare hour the first word of a line arises in their midst and strides out of them.

But all my lines came about otherwise, so they aren't poetry. And when I wrote my play, how mistaken I was. Was I an imitator and a fool that I needed a third person to tell about the fate of two people who were making life difficult for each other? How easily I fell into the trap. And I ought to have known that this third person, who haunts all lives and literatures, this specter of a third who never was, has no meaning, that he must be denied. He is one of the pretexts of nature, which is always striving to divert people's attention from her deepest mysteries. He is the screen behind which a drama plays itself out. He is the noise at the entrance to the voiceless silence of a genuine conflict. One might think that up to then it had been too difficult to speak of the two the play is about; the third, precisely because he is so unreal, is the easy part of the task, they could all do him. Right at the beginning of their plays one notices the writers' impatience to get to this third, they can hardly wait. As soon as he arrives everything's fine. But how boring if he's delayed, nothing can happen without him, everything stands, stops, waits. But what if the play were to stay with this building up and standing around? What, Mr. Dramatist, and you, Public that knows life, what if he were to get lost, this popular playboy or this presumptuous young man who unlocks every marriage like a duplicate key? What if, for example, the Devil had made off with him? Let's suppose that. Suddenly one notices the artificial emptiness of theaters, they are walled up like dangerous holes, only the moths tumble from the railings of the loges through the hollow, yawning space. Dramatists no longer enjoy their elegant villas. All the public snoops search on their behalf in remote parts of the world for that which is irreplaceable, the action itself.

And yet these dramatists live among people, not these "thirds," but the two about whom so incredibly much could be said, about whom nothing has ever yet been said, although they suffer and act and don't know how to help themselves.

It's ridiculous. Here I sit in my little room, I, Brigge, who have got to be twenty-eight years old and about whom no one knows. I sit here and am nothing. And yet this nothing begins to think and thinks, up five flights of stairs, these thoughts on a gray Paris afternoon:

Is it possible, this nothing thinks, that one has not yet seen, recognized, and said anything real and important? Is it possible that one has had thousands of years of time to look, reflect, and write down, and that one has let the millennia pass away like a school recess in which one eats one's sandwich and an apple?

Yes, it is possible.

Is it possible that in spite of inventions and progress, in spite of culture, religion, and worldly wisdom, that one has remained on the surface of life? Is it possible that one has even covered this surface, which would at least have been something, with an incredibly dull slipcover, so that it looks like living-room furniture during the summer vacation?

Yes, it is possible.

Is it possible that the whole history of the world has been misunderstood? Is it possible that the past is false because one has always spoken of its masses, as if one was telling about a coming together of many people, instead of telling about the one person they were standing around, because he was alien and died?

Yes, it is possible.

Is it possible that one believed one had to make up for everything that happened before one was born? Is it possible one would have to remind every single person that he arose from all earlier people so that he would know it, and not let himself be talked out of it by the others, who see it differently?

Yes, it is possible.

Is it possible that all these people know very precisely a past that never was? Is it possible that everything real is nothing to them; that their life takes its course, connected to nothing, like a clock in an empty room?

Yes, it is possible.

Is it possible that one knows nothing about girls, who are nevertheless alive? Is it possible that one says "the women," "the children," "the boys," and doesn't suspect (in spite of all one's education doesn't suspect) that for the longest time these words have no longer had a plural, but only innumerable singulars?

Yes, it is possible.

Is it possible that there are people who say "God" and think it is something they have in common? Just look at two schoolboys: one buys himself a knife, and the same day his neighbor buys one just like it. And after a week they show each other their knives and it turns out that they bear only the remotest resemblance to each other—so differently have they developed in different hands. (Well, the mother of one of them says, if you boys always have to wear everything out right away.) Ah, so: is it possible to believe that one could have a God without using him?

Yes, it is possible.

But if all this is possible, has even an appearance of possibility—then for heaven's sake something has to happen. The first person who comes along, the one who has had this disquieting thought, must begin to accomplish some of what has been missed; even if he is just anyone, not the most suitable person: there is simply no one else there. This young, irrelevant foreigner, Brigge, will have to sit himself down five flights up and write, day and night, he will just have to write, and that will be that.

I must at that time have been twelve, or at most thirteen. My father had taken me along to Urnekloster. I don't know what moved him to seek out his father-in-law. The two had not seen each other for years, since my mother's death, and my father had never been in the old castle, to which Count Brahe had withdrawn only later. I never saw the remarkable house afterwards; when my grandfather died it passed into strange hands. As I find it again in my retrieved childhood memory it is not a building; it is completely divided up in me: a room here, a room there, and a piece of corridor that does not connect these two rooms but is preserved by itself, as a fragment. Everything is scattered around in me in this way: the rooms, the staircases that unrolled downwards with such great complexity, and other narrow, spiral staircases whose darkness one negotiated like blood in the veins; the tower rooms, the balconies suspended high up, the unexpected high platforms onto which a small door pushed one out: all that is in me and will never cease to be in me. It is as if the image of this house had fallen into me from an infinite height and shattered on my ground.

The only thing that is preserved in my heart, so it seems to me, is the great hall in which we usually gathered for dinner every evening at seven. I never saw this hall in daylight, I don't even remember whether it had windows or what they looked out on; every time, whenever the family came in, candles were burning in the heavy sconces, and within a few minutes one forgot the time of day and everything one had seen outside. This high, as I imagine vaulted space overpowered everything: with its darkling height, its never quite visible corners, it sucked all images out of one without giving one a tangible substitute in return. One sat there as if lamed: completely without will, without consciousness, without desire, without resistance. One was like a blank spot. I remember that this crushing state at first almost made me sick to my stomach, a kind of seasickness, which I overcame only by sticking out my leg until my foot touched the knee of my father, who was sitting opposite me. Only later did it occur to me that he seemed to understand, or at least tolerate, this remarkable behavior, although the relationship between us was almost cool and could not explain such a gesture. But it was this gentle touch that gave me the strength to hold out during the long mealtimes. And after several weeks of desperate endurance I had, with a child's almost unlimited adaptability, become so accustomed to the uncanniness of these gatherings that it was no longer a strain to sit at table for two hours; now they even passed relatively quickly, because I occupied myself by studying those present.

My grandfather called them the family, and I heard the others use this word too, which was quite arbitrary. For although these four people were distantly related to each other, they did not in the least belong together. The uncle who sat beside me was an old man whose hard and burned face exhibited several black spots, the result, as I learned, of an exploding powder charge; surly and malcontent as he was, he had taken retirement as Major and was performing alchemical experiments in a room of the castle I did not know, and was also, as I heard the servants say, in contact with a supply house that once or twice a year sent him corpses with which he locked himself up for days and nights together, and which he dissected and prepared in a secret way so they resisted decomposition. Opposite him was the place of Fräulein Mathilde Brahe. She was a person of indefinite age, a distant cousin of my mother, and nothing was known about her other than that she maintained a quite active correspondence with an Austrian spiritualist who called himself Baron Nolde and to whom she was completely devoted, so that she did not undertake the smallest thing without seeking his agreement beforehand, or rather something like his blessing. She was at that time extraordinarily corpulent, of a soft, indolent fullness that had been, so to speak, inattentively poured into her bright, loose-fitting clothes. Her gestures were vague and fatigued, and her eyes constantly tearing.

But nevertheless there was something in her that reminded me of my gentle and slender mother. The longer I observed her, I found in her face all the fine and soft features that I had never been able to remember rightly after my mother's death; only now, seeing Mathilde Brahe every day, did I recognize what the deceased looked like; indeed, I knew it perhaps for the first time. Only now, out of hundreds and hundreds of details, did a picture of the departed form in me, that picture that accompanies me everywhere. Later I realized that all the details that composed the features of my mother were actually present in Fräulein Brahe's face—they were only stretched apart, distorted, and no longer in harmony with each other, as if some strange face had pushed its way in between.

Beside this lady sat the small son of a cousin, a boy of about my own age but smaller and more delicate. His thin, pale neck rose out of the fine folds of a ruff and disappeared beneath a long chin. His lips were narrow and firmly closed, his nostrils trembled gently, and only one of his fine dark brown eyes moved. It sometimes looked over at me calmly and sadly, while the other eye always remained directed at the same corner, as if it had been sold and was no longer involved.

At the upper end of the table stood my grandfather's enormous armchair, which a servant who had no other function pushed up to the table as he sat down, and in which the old man occupied only a small space. There were people who called this dominating and hard-of-hearing old gentleman Excellency and Court Marshal, others gave him the title of General. And he certainly possessed all those honors, but it had been so long since he had occupied any official position that these appellations were hardly any longer intelligible. It seemed to me altogether that no specific name could be applied to this personage who was at certain moments so sharp, and yet distracted again and again. I could never make up my mind to call him grandfather, although from time to time he was friendly towards me, indeed even called me over to him and would try to give my name a jocular emphasis. The whole family behaved toward the Count with a mixture of reverence and shyness, but only little Erik lived in a certain confidential relationship with the old master of the house; his moving eye had at times quick glances of understanding with him, which were just as quickly returned by his grandfather; one could also see the two of them sometimes appear at the end of the deep gallery during the long afternoons and observe how, hand in hand, they walked past the dark old portraits without speaking, evidently communicating with each other in some other way.

I found myself almost the whole day long on the grounds and outside in the beech woods or on the heath; fortunately there were dogs at Urnekloster who accompanied me. Here and there was a tenant's house or a dairy farm where I could get milk and bread and fruit, and I believe that I enjoyed my freedom in rather carefree fashion, at least in the weeks that followed, without letting myself become anxious about the evening gatherings. I spoke with almost no one, for it was my joy to be alone; I only had brief conversations now and then with the dogs: with them I was on the best of terms. Silence was, moreover, a kind of family trait; I knew it from my father, and it did not surprise me that during the evening meal almost nothing was said.

In the first days after our arrival, however, Mathilde Brahe was extremely loquacious. She asked my father about earlier acquaintances in foreign cities, she remembered remote impressions, she moved herself to tears by calling up women friends who had died and a certain young man who, she intimated, had loved her without her caring to return his insistent but hopeless affection. My father listened politely, nodded his head sympathetically here and there, answering when he had to. The Count, at the head of the table, constantly smiled with drawn-down lips. His face appeared larger than usual, it was as if he were wearing a mask. He sometimes spoke up, though his voice was directed at no particular person; and although it was very soft it could be heard throughout the entire hall. It had something of the regular, indifferent beat of a clock; the silence around it seemed to have its own empty resonance, the same for every syllable.

Count Brahe considered it a special courtesy to my father to speak of his deceased wife, my mother. He called her Countess Sybille, and all his sentences concluded as if he were asking about her. Indeed it seemed to me, I don't know why, as if it were a question of a very young girl dressed in white who could come among us at any moment. I heard him speak of "our little Anna Sophie" in the same tone. And when, one day, I asked about this girl, who appeared to be a special favorite of Grandfather's, I discovered that he was referring to the daughter of the High Chancellor Reventlow, once the morganatic spouse of Frederick the Fourth, who had been resting at Roskilde for nearly a century and a half. The passage of time played no role at all for him, death was a minor incident that he totally ignored. People he had once taken into his memory *existed*, and against that their dying could not have the least effect. Several years later, after the old gentleman's death, one recalled how he had felt the future with the same stubbornness. He was once supposed to have spoken to a certain young woman about her sons, of the travels of one of these sons in particular, while the young woman, just in the third month of her first pregnancy, sat almost senseless from fear and horror beside the incessantly talking old man.

But it began with my laughing. Yes, I laughed out loud and couldn't stop. One evening Mathilde Brahe was missing. Yet the old, almost completely blind servant, when he came to her place, held out the serving dishes. He stayed like that for a while, then went on, satisfied and with dignity, as if everything had been quite in order. I had observed this scene, and at the moment when I saw it did not find it in the least comic. But a little later, just as I put a morsel in my mouth, laughter sprang to my head with such rapidity that I swallowed the wrong way and caused a great uproar. And though this situation was troublesome to me myself, and notwithstanding my attempts in all possible ways to be serious, this laughter continued to erupt spasmodically and maintained complete control over me.

My father, as if to cover my behavior, asked in his broad, subdued voice: "Is Mathilde ill?" Grandfather smiled in the way he had and answered with a sentence that I, occupied as I was with myself, did not pay attention to but that went something like: No, she just doesn't want to meet Christine. So I also did not see it as the effect of these words that my neighbor, the brown Major, stood up and, with an indistinctly murmured excuse and a bow to the old Count, left the hall. I only noticed that behind the back of the master of the house he turned around once more in the doorway and made motions with his hand and head to little Erik, and suddenly to my great astonishment to me as well, as if he were asking us to follow him. I was so surprised that my laughter ceased to distress me. For the rest, I paid no further attention to the Major; I found him unpleasant, and noticed that little Erik ignored him too.

The meal dragged on as always, and we had just got to the dessert when my glance was caught and absorbed by a movement occurring in the background of the hall, in the semi-darkness. Gradually a door opened, a door I had thought was always closed, about which I had been told that it led to the mezzanine floor, and now, as I looked on with an entirely new feeling of curiosity and dismay, in the darkness of the doorway a slender lady in a bright dress appeared and slowly came toward us. I don't know whether I made a movement or uttered a sound, the noise of an overturning chair forced me to tear my glance away from the remarkable figure and I saw my father, who had jumped up and now, his face deathly pale, with clenched fists hanging, went up to the lady. Quite undisturbed by this scene she kept coming toward us, step by step, and she was already not very far from the Count's place when he abruptly stood up, grabbed my father by the arm, and pulling him back to the table held him there as the strange lady, slowly and indifferently, walked past through the now open space step by step, through indescribable stillness in which only a glass tinkled tremblingly, and disappeared through a door in the opposite wall. At this moment I noticed that it was little Erik who, with a deep bow, closed the door behind the stranger.

I was the only person who had remained sitting at the table; I had sunk down so low in my chair that it seemed to me I could never climb up again by myself. For a while I saw without seeing. Then I remembered my father, and became aware that the old man was still holding him firmly by the arm. My father's face was angry, filled with blood, but my grandfather, whose fingers were gripping my father's arm like a white claw, was smiling his mask-like smile. I then heard him saying something, syllable by syllable, but could not make out the sense of his words. Yet they sank deep into my hearing, for about two years ago I found them at the bottom of my memory, and since then I know them. He said: "You are violent, Chamberlain, and impolite. Why don't you let people go about their business?" "Who is that?" shouted my father, interrupting. "Someone who has a perfect right to be here. No stranger. Christine Brahe." That remarkable thin stillness again intervened, and the glass again began to tremble. But then my father tore himself loose and rushed out of the hall.

I heard him pacing up and down all night in his room, for I could not sleep either. But suddenly toward morning I awoke from something like sleep and with a horror that paralyzed me to the heart saw something white sitting by my bed. My desperation finally gave me the strength to stick my head under the covers, and there I began to cry from fear and helplessness. Suddenly it became cool and bright above my weeping eyes; I pressed them shut over my tears so as not to have to see anything. But the voice that now spoke to me from quite close came mild and cloying toward my face, and I recognized it: it was Fräulein Mathilde's voice. I calmed down immediately, but even when I was quite calm still let myself be comforted. I felt that this kindness was too weak, but nevertheless I enjoyed it and thought I had somehow deserved it. "Aunt," I said finally, and tried to pull together in her blurred face the features of my mother, "Aunt, who was the lady?"

"Ah," Fräulein Brahe answered with a sigh that I found comical, "an unhappy woman, my child, an unhappy woman."

On the morning of that day I noticed some servants in a room busily packing. I thought we would be leaving, I found it quite natural that we would now be leaving. Perhaps that was my father's purpose too. I never found out what motivated him to stay on at Urnekloster after that evening. But we did not leave. We stayed on in this house for eight weeks, or nine, we bore the pressure of its peculiarities, and we saw Christine Brahe three more times.

At that time I knew nothing of her history. I did not know that she had died long, long before, giving birth to her second child, bearing a son who grew up to a fearful and cruel fate—I did not know that she was a dead person. But my father knew. Had he, who was passionate and disposed to consistency and clarity, wanted to force himself to see this adventure through, composed and without asking questions? I saw, without understanding it, how he struggled with himself, I experienced it without understanding how he finally got hold of himself.

That happened when we saw Christine Brahe for the last time. On this occasion Fräulein Mathilde appeared at table, but she was different than before. As in the first days after our arrival she spoke incessantly and erratically, continually becoming confused, and at the same time there was in her a physical restlessness that forced her to fiddle constantly with something in her hair or on her dress—until she unexpectedly jumped up with a high, lamenting cry and disappeared.

At the same moment my gaze involuntarily turned to that same door, and truly: Christine Brahe walked in. My neighbor, the Major, made a short, brusque gesture that transmitted itself to my body, but obviously he no longer had the energy to get up. His old, brown, spotted face turned from one to another, his mouth was open, and his tongue twisted behind his ruined teeth; then suddenly this face was gone and his gray head lay on the table, his arms lying as if in pieces over and under it, and from somewhere a withered, spotted hand appeared and trembled.

And now Christine Brahe walked past, step by step, slowly, like an ill person, through indescribable stillness into which only a single whimpering sound echoed like that of an old dog. But then there appeared to the left of the large silver swan filled with daffodils the great mask of the old man, with its gray smile. He raised his wine-glass toward my father. And now I saw how my father, just as Christine Brahe passed behind his chair, reached for his glass and raised it like something very heavy a hand's breadth above the table.

And that very night we left.

Bibliothèque Nationale

I am sitting and reading a poet. There are many people in the hall, but one doesn't feel them. They are in their books. Sometimes they move in the pages, like people who are sleeping and who turn over between two dreams. Ah, how good it is to be among people reading. Why are they not always so? You can go up to one and touch him gently: he feels nothing. And if you gently bump into your neighbor as you stand up, and excuse yourself, he nods toward the side on which he hears your voice, his face turns to you and does not see you, and his hair is like the hair of a person asleep. How good it feels. And I sit and have a poet. What a destiny. There are now perhaps three hundred people in the hall who are reading; but it is impossible for every single one of them to have a poet. (God knows what they have.) There aren't three hundred poets. But look, what a destiny. I, perhaps the most wretched among these readers, a foreigner: I have a poet. Although I am poor. Although my suit, which I wear every day, is beginning to show through in certain places, although this or that objection might be made against my shoes. Of course my collar is clean, my shirt too, and as I am I could go into any café, possibly even on the grand boulevards, and confidently thrust my hand out to a plate of cakes and take something. No one would take this amiss or scold me or throw me out, for it is still a hand of the better classes, a hand that is washed four or five times a day. There is nothing under the nails, the index finger has no inkstain, and the wrists especially are spotless. Poor people don't wash up that far, that's a well-known fact. So one can draw certain conclusions from their cleanliness. One does, too. In shops one draws them. But there are a few lives, on the Boulevard Saint-Michel for instance and in the rue Racine, that don't let themselves be put off, that don't give a damn about their wrists. They look at me and know. They know that I am really one of them, that I am only playing a little comedy. It is, after all, carnival time. And they don't want to spoil my fun; they just grin a little and wink. No one sees it. Otherwise, they treat me like a gentleman. But if somebody happens to be near, then they even grovel, act as if I were wearing a fur coat and my car was following along behind me. Sometimes I give them two sous and tremble lest they refuse them, but they take them. And everything would be in order if they didn't grin and wink a little again. Who are these people? What do they want from me? Are they waiting for me? How do they recognize me? It's true my beard looks somewhat neglected, and it is barely vaguely reminiscent of their sick, old, faded beards that always impressed me. But don't I have the right to neglect my beard? Many busy people do, and it would never occur to anyone to immediately lump them together with the outcasts on that account. For it is clear to me that these people are outcasts, not just beggars. No, they're really not beggars; one must discriminate. They are trash, husks of people spat out by fate. Damp from the saliva of fate they stick to a wall, to a lamppost, to an advertising pillar, or they slowly ooze down the street, leaving a dark, dirty trace behind. What in the world did that old woman want from me who, carrying the drawer of a night table in which a few buttons and needles were rolling around, had crept out of some hole or other? Why did she always walk beside me and look at me? As if she were trying to recognize me with her watery eyes that looked as if some sick person had spat green slime into her bleeding lids? And how, that other time, did that small gray woman come to stand for a quarter of an hour beside me before a shop window while showing me an old, long pencil that protruded with infinite slowness from her filthy, closed hands? I acted as if I were looking at the goods displayed and didn't notice anything. But she knew I had seen her, she knew I was standing there and wondering what she was really doing. For I understood quite well that it could not be a question of the pencil: I felt that it was a sign, a sign for the initiated, a sign that the outcasts recognize; I felt she was indicating to me that I had to go somewhere or do something. And the oddest thing was that I could not shake off the feeling that there really was a certain appointment to which this sign belonged, and that this scene was basically something I ought to have expected.

That was two weeks ago. But now almost no day passes without such an encounter. Not just at twilight; at noon in the most crowded streets it happens that suddenly a little man or an old woman appears, nods, shows me something, and vanishes again as if everything that was necessary had been done. It's possible that one day it will occur to them to come as far as my room, they certainly know where I live, and they will arrange it so the concierge does not stop them. But here, my friends, here I am safe from you. You need a special card to enter this hall. This card is my advantage over you. I walk through the streets somewhat cautiously, as one may imagine, but finally I am in front of a glass door, open it as if I were at home, show my card at the next door (exactly as you show me your objects, only with the difference that the people here understand me and comprehend what I say), and then I am among these books, taken away from you as if I had died, and sit and read a poet.

You don't know what that is, a poet? Verlaine . . . Nothing? No memory? No. You didn't distinguish him among those you knew? You make no distinctions, I know. But I am reading another poet, one who does not live in Paris, a quite different one.[5] A poet who has a silent house in the mountains. Who sounds like a bell in pure air. A happy poet, who talks about his window and the glass doors of his bookcase, doors that pensively reflect a cherished, lonely distance. He is exactly the poet I would have wanted to become; for he knows so much about girls, and I would also have known much about them. He knows about girls who lived a hundred years ago; it no longer matters that they are dead, for he knows everything. And that is the main thing. He pronounces their names, those soft, thinly-written names with the old-fashioned loops in the long letters and the grown-up names of their older friends, in which there is already a very small echo of fate, a very little disappointment and death. Perhaps their faded letters and the separated pages of their diaries in which are noted summer outings and birthdays are already lying in a drawer of the poet's mahogany desk. Or it may be that in the bombé wardrobe at the back of his bedroom there is a drawer in which their spring dresses are preserved; white dresses that were worn for the first time around Easter, dresses of speckled tulle that really belong to the summer one could not wait for. Oh what a happy fate, to sit in the quiet room of an inherited house among nothing but calm, settled things and to hear in the casual light-green garden outside the first tentative notes of the titmouse, and the village clock in the distance. To sit there and look at a warm strip of afternoon sun and to know much about girls of the past and to be a poet. And to think that I too would have become such a poet if I had been able to live somewhere, anywhere in the world, in one of the many closed-up country houses that no one bothers about. I would only

---

5   Francis Jammes.

have needed one room (the light room in the gable). I would have lived in it with my old things, the family portraits, the books. And I would have had an easy chair and flowers and dogs, and a sturdy stick for the stony paths. And nothing else. Only a book bound in yellowish, ivory-colored leather with an old flowery pattern as endpaper; I would have written in that, I would have written much, for I would have had many thoughts, and memories of many things. But it has turned out differently, God alone knows why. My old furniture is rotting in a barn in which I was allowed to put it, and I myself, my God, I have no roof over me and it rains into my eyes.

Sometimes I walk past small shops, perhaps in the rue de Seine. Dealers in antiques or engravings, or small antiquarian booksellers with overflowing display windows. No one ever goes in, it's obvious that they don't do any business. But if one looks inside they are sitting, sitting and reading, unconcerned; not worried about tomorrow, not anxious about success, have a dog sitting before them, happy, or a cat that makes the silence still larger as it slinks along the rows of books as if it were flicking the names off the spines.

Ah, if that were enough: I would sometimes wish to buy such a full display window and sit behind it with a dog for twenty years.

It is good to say it aloud: "Nothing has happened." Once more: "Nothing has happened." Does it help?

That my stove has smoked yet again and I had to go out is really no misfortune. That I feel worn out and chilled means nothing. That I have run around in the streets the whole day is my own fault. I could just as well have sat in the Louvre. Or no, that I couldn't. There are certain people there trying to warm themselves. They sit on the velvet banquettes, their feet standing beside each other on the heating grilles like big empty boots. They are extremely modest men, who are grateful if the guards in the dark uniforms with many medals tolerate them. But when I come in they grin. Grin and give a little nod. And then, if I walk back and forth in front of the paintings, they keep their eyes on me, always on me, always their unmoved, rheumy eyes. So it was good that I didn't go to the Louvre. I have always been on the move. God knows in how many cities, neighborhoods, cemeteries, bridges, and passageways. Somewhere I saw a man pushing a vegetable cart before him. He was shouting "Chou-fleur, Chou-fleur," the "fleur" with a peculiarly mournful "eu." Walking beside him was a squarish ugly woman who poked him from time to time. And whenever she poked him, he shouted. Sometimes he also shouted on his own, but then it was useless, and he had to shout again immediately afterward because he was in front of a house that bought. Have I already said that he was blind? No? Well, he was blind. He was blind and shouted. I'm simplifying when I say that, I'm suppressing the cart he was pushing, I'm acting as if I hadn't noticed that he was shouting "cauliflower." But is that important? And even if it were important, isn't what really matters what the whole incident meant to me? I saw an old man who was blind and shouted. That's what I saw. Saw.

Will people believe that such houses exist? No, they will say I'm making it up. This time it is true, nothing left out, of course nothing added, either. Where would I have got it from? One knows that I am poor. One knows it. Houses? But, to be precise, they were houses that were no longer there. Houses that had been torn down from top to bottom. What *was* there were the other houses that had stood beside them, high neighboring houses. They were obviously in danger of collapsing since everything next door had been removed, for a whole scaffolding of long, tarred tree-masts had been rammed diagonally between the exposed walls and the area of debris on the ground. I don't know whether I have already said that these are the walls I mean. But not the outer wall of the houses still standing (as one would have had to assume), but the interior wall of the former houses. One saw its inner side. One saw on the various floors the walls of rooms to which the wallpaper still clung, here and there the stump of a floor or ceiling. Beside the walls of the rooms there was along the entire wall a dirty white space, through which crawled in indescribably repulsive, worm-soft, so to speak digesting movements the open, rust-spotted gutter of lavatory pipes. Of the paths taken by illuminating gas gray, dusty spaces remained at the edge of the ceilings, and here and there they bent around quite unexpectedly on the floor and ran into the colored wall and into a hole that was black and had been ruthlessly punched out. But the most unforgettable things were the walls themselves. The tenacious life of these rooms had not let itself be stamped out. It was still there, it hung on the remaining nails, it stood on the hand's breadth of floor that was left, it had shriveled into the stubs of the corners, where there was still a little bit of interior space. One could see it in the paint that had slowly, year after year, transformed this space: blue into moldy green, green into gray, and yellow into an old, stale white that was putrefying. But it was also in the fresher places that had been preserved behind mirrors, pictures, and cupboards, for it had drawn and redrawn their outlines and had also, along with spiders and dust, been in these hidden places that now lay exposed. It was in every scraped-off strip, it was in the damp bubbles at the bottom edge of the wallpaper, it fluttered in the hanging shreds and sweated from the nasty spots that had formed long ago. And from these walls that had been blue, green, and yellow, framed by the trusses of the destroyed inner walls, the air of these lives stood out, the tenacious, sluggish, moldy air that no wind had yet dispersed. There remained the noons and the illnesses and the exhalations of the smoke of years, and the sweat that breaks out in the armpits and makes clothes heavy, and the bad breath of mouths and the oily smell of yeasty feet. In it remained the sharpness of urine and the burning of soot and gray potato odor and the heavy, smooth stink of rancid fat. The sweet, long smell of neglected infants was in it, and the odor of fear from children going off to school, and the sultriness from the beds of pubescent boys. And much had mingled with all this that had risen from below, from the abyss of the narrow, transpiring street, and other smells that had trickled down from above with the rain, which over cities is not clean. And many had been brought by the weak, tame house-winds that always stay in the same street, and there were many other odors whose origin one did not know. I said, didn't I, that all the walls had been pulled down except for the last? Now this is the wall I have been speaking about all this time. One will say that I stood before it for a long while; but I will take an oath on it that as soon as I recognized the wall I began to run. For that is the terrible thing, that I recognized it. I recognize all these things here, and that is why it enters me so readily: it is at home in me.

After all this I was rather exhausted, one might well say debilitated, and so it was too much for me that he too had to be waiting for me. He was waiting in the small crémerie where I wanted to have two fried eggs; I was hungry, I hadn't gotten around to eating all day. But now I couldn't eat anything either. Before the eggs were ready

I was driven out again into the streets, which ran toward me quite viscous with people. For it was Carnival and evening, and people had all the time in the world and were drifting around and rubbing up against one another. And their faces were full of the light coming from the carnival booths, and laughter welled from their mouths like pus from open sores. They laughed more and more and pressed ever tighter together the more impatiently I tried to move forward. A woman's scarf somehow stuck to me, I dragged her behind me, and people stopped me and laughed, and I felt that I should laugh too, but I couldn't. Someone threw a handful of confetti in my eyes, and it burned like a whip. On the corners people were wedged firmly together, one shoved into another, and there was no moving on in them, only a gentle, soft up and down, as if they were copulating standing. But although they were standing and I, at the edge of the street where there were gaps in the crowds, was running toward them like a madman, it was really they who were moving and I wasn't stirring. For nothing changed; when I looked up, I always saw the same houses on one side and the carnival booths on the other. Perhaps too everything was standing still and it was only a dizziness in me and in them that seemed to make everything spin around. I had no time to think about it, I was heavy with sweat, and a numbing pain was circling in me as if something too large was circulating along with my blood, stretching the veins wherever it went. And I felt that the air had long since given out and that I was only breathing in exhalations that made my lungs stop.

But now it's over, I have survived it. I am sitting in my room near the lamp; it is a little chilly, for I don't dare try the stove; what if it were to smoke and I would have to go out again? I sit and think: if I were not poor I would rent another room, a room with furniture that was not so worn out, not so full of earlier tenants as this one is. At first it was really hard for me to lay my head back in this armchair, for in its green covering there is a kind of smeary gray hollow into which all heads seem to fit. For quite a long time I took the precaution of putting a handkerchief behind my head, but now I'm too tired to; I have discovered that it works without it and that the small indentation is made precisely for my head, as if to measure. But if I were not poor I would first of all buy a good stove, and I would heat with pure, hard wood that comes from the mountains, and not these hopeless charcoal briquettes whose fumes make breathing so anxious and the head so confused. And then there would have to be someone to clean up without bothersome noise and take care of the fire the way I need it done; for often when I have to kneel for a quarter of an hour before the stove shaking the embers, the skin on my forehead stretched by the fire and the heat in my open eyes, I exhaust all the energy I have for the whole day, and if I then go out among people, they of course have it easy. Sometimes, when there are great crowds, I would take a cab, ride around, I would eat in a Duval . . . and no longer creep into the crémeries[6] . . . Whether he too would have been in a Duval? No. He would not have been allowed to wait for me there. They don't let dying people into those better places. Dying people? I'm now sitting in my room; I can try to think calmly about what I encountered. It's good not to leave anything uncertain. So I walked in, and at first saw only that the table I often used to sit at was occupied by someone else. I said hello in the direction of the small counter, ordered, and sat down at the next table. But then I felt him, although he did not stir. What I felt was precisely his lack of movement, and comprehended it

---

6   Crémerie: a simple restaurant; Duval: a better sort.

in a flash. The connection between us was established, and I knew he was petrified with horror. I knew that the horror had paralyzed him, horror at something that was going on inside him. Perhaps some vessel was breaking in him, perhaps a poison he had long feared was just now entering the chambers of his heart, perhaps a large tumor was rising in his brain like a sun that was transforming the world for him. With indescribable effort I forced myself to look over at him, for I was still hoping it was all my imagining. But what happened was that I jumped up and rushed out; for I had not been mistaken. He was sitting there in a heavy black winter coat, and his gray, taut face hung down into a woolen scarf. His mouth was closed as if it had fallen shut with great force, but it was not possible to say whether his eyes still saw: smoky gray spectacles, misted over, covered them and were trembling slightly. His nostrils flared, and over his temples the long hair from which everything had been withdrawn wilted as from excessive heat. His ears were long, yellow, with large shadows behind them. Yes, he knew that he was now leaving everything, not just people. Another instant and everything will have lost its meaning, and this table, and the cup, and the chair he is gripping tightly, all the everyday and closest things, will have become incomprehensible, alien and heavy. Thus he sat there and waited for it to be over. And no longer resisted.

But I am still resisting. I resist although I know that my heart is already hanging out of me and that I can no longer live, even if my tormentors desist. I tell myself: nothing has happened, and yet I could only have understood that man because something is going on in me as well, something that is beginning to distance and separate me from everything. How horrified I always was when I heard it said of someone who was dying: he could no longer recognize anyone. Then I would imagine a lonely face raising itself from its pillows and searching, searching for something familiar, searching for something that had once been seen, but there was nothing there. If my fear were not so great I would console myself by saying that it is not impossible to see everything differently and still go on living. But I am afraid, I am deathly afraid of this change. I still have not become accustomed to this world, which to me seems good. What should I do in another one? I would so gladly remain among the meanings that have become dear to me, and if something does have to change, I would at least like to be allowed to live among dogs, who have a related world and the same things.

For a while yet I can write all this down and say it. But a day will come when my hand will be far from me, and if I bid it write, it will write words I do not intend. The time of the other interpretation will begin, and no word will remain with the next, and every meaning will dissolve like clouds and come down like water. For all my fear I am like someone standing before something great, and I remember that it often used to be like this in me, before I began to write. But this time I shall be written. I am the impress that will transform itself. Oh it wants just a little, and I could understand and approve of it all. Only a step, and my profound misery would be bliss. But I cannot take this step, I have fallen and can no longer get up, because I am broken. Yet I have always believed that some help would come. That which I have prayed for evening after evening lies before me in my own handwriting. I have copied it down from the books in which I found it so that it would be quite close to me, arisen out of my hand as something that is my own. And now I want to write it down yet once more, kneeling here before my table I want to write it down; for that way I will have it longer than if I read it, and every word lasts and has time to die away.

"Mécontent de tous et mécontent de moi, je voudrais bien me ra-
cheter et m'engorgeuillir un peu dans le silence et la solitude de la nuit.
Âmes de ceux que j'ai aimés, âmes de ceux que j'ai chantés, fortifiez-
moi, soutenez-moi, éloignez de moi le mensonge et les vapeurs corrup-
trices du monde; et vous, Seigneur mon Dieu! accordez moi la grâce de
produire quelques beaux vers qui me prouvent à moi-même que je ne
suis pas le dernier des hommes, que je ne suis pas inférieur à ceux que
je méprise."[7]

"The children of loose and despised people, who were the lowest in
the land. Now I have come to be their harpsong and must be their
tale.

. . . they have made a path over me . . .

. . . it was so easy for them to damage me that they had no need of aid.

. . . but now poureth over me out of my soul, and the time of misery
hath seized hold of me.

At night my bones are bored through in every wise; and those that
hunt me do not lay themselves down to sleep.

Through the force of the power I am clothed this way and that; I am
belted as with the hole in my garment . . .

My entrails boil and do not cease; the time of misery hath fallen
upon me . . .

My harp has become a lament, and my flute a weeping."

---

7   "Dissatisfied with everyone, dissatisfied with myself, I would like to re-
deem myself and find a little pride in the silence and solitude of the night.
Souls of those I have loved, souls of those I have sung, strengthen me, sustain
me, remove from me the lies and corrupting vapors of the world; and you,
my Lord God, grant me the grace to produce some fine verses that will prove
to me that I am not the least of men, that I am not inferior to those I scorn."
(Baudelaire, from "One o'clock in the morning," *Poems in Prose*—trans.)

The doctor did not understand me. Nothing. It was also hard to talk about. They wanted to try electric shock therapy. Good. I was given a piece of paper: I was to be at the Salpêtrière at one o'clock. I was there. I had to pass some long barracks and go through several courtyards, in which here and there people with white hoods were standing around like prisoners under the leafless trees. Finally I entered a long, corridor-like room that along one side had four windows of dull greenish glass, separated one from another by wide black sections of wall. A wooden bench ran underneath along the entire wall, and those who knew me were sitting on this bench, waiting. Yes, they were all there. When I had become accustomed to the twilight in the room, I noticed that among those who were sitting there shoulder to shoulder in an endless row there might also be several other people, little people, tradespeople, servants, and carters. Down at the narrow end of the corridor two corpulent women, presumably concierges, had spread themselves out on individual chairs, chatting. I looked at the clock: it was five minutes to one. Well, in five, let's say ten minutes it would be my turn; that wasn't so bad. The air was stifling, heavy, full of clothes and breath. At a certain place the strong, intensifying coolness of ether came through the crack of a door. I began to pace up and down. The thought came to me that I had been ordered here, among these people, in this overfilled, general office hour. It was, so to speak, the first public confirmation that I belonged to the outcasts; had the doctor seen that in me? But I had paid my visit in a passably good suit, I had sent in my card. Nevertheless, he must have found it out somehow, perhaps I had betrayed myself. Well, since it was a fact I didn't find it so bad; the people were sitting silently and paying no attention to me. Several were in pain, and moved one leg back and forth a little to bear it more easily. Some men had placed their heads in the palms of their hands, others slept with heavy, submerged faces. A fat man with a red, swollen neck sat bent over forward, staring at the floor, and from time to time spat with a splat on a spot that seemed to him suitable. A child was sobbing in a corner; it had drawn up its long, emaciated legs on a bench and embraced them with its arms, pressing them to itself as if it had to take leave of them. A small pale woman, who was sitting with a crepe hat decorated with round black flowers askew on her hair, had the grimace of a smile around her bloodless lips, but her sore eyelids were constantly tearing. Not far from her a girl with a smooth round face and protruding, expressionless eyes had been put; her mouth was open so that one saw her white, slimy gums and old, rotted teeth. And there were lots of bandages. Bandages that wound around the entire head layer upon layer until only a single eye was left that no longer belonged to anyone. Bandages that concealed and bandages that revealed what was underneath them. Bandages that had been opened and on which now, as on a dirty bed, there lay a hand that was no longer a hand; and a bound-up leg stood out from the row, as large as a whole person. I paced up and down, making an effort to be calm. I concentrated a lot on the opposite wall. I noticed that it contained a number of doors and did not go all the way up to the ceiling, so that this corridor was not entirely blocked off from rooms that must lie on the other side. I looked at the clock; I had been walking up and down for an hour. A while later the doctors arrived. First a couple of young people who walked past with indifferent faces, finally the one I had been to see, in light-colored gloves, a shiny silk top hat, and a spotless topcoat. When he saw me he lifted his hat slightly and smiled distractedly. I now had some hopes of being called right away, but another hour passed. I can't remember how

I spent it. It passed. An old man in a soiled apron came out, a kind of attendant, and touched me on the shoulder. I went into one of the adjoining rooms. The doctor and the young people were sitting around a table and looked at me, I was given a chair. So. Now I was supposed to tell them what was bothering me. And as briefly as possible, *s'il vous plaît*. For the gentlemen did not have much time. I had a strange feeling. The young people sat and looked at me with the superior professional curiosity they had learned. The doctor I knew stroked his black goatee and smiled distractedly. I thought I would burst into tears, but heard myself saying in French: "I have already had the honor, sir, of telling you everything I could. If you think it necessary to inform these gentlemen, you are fully prepared after our interview to do so in your own words, while it is very difficult for me." The doctor rose with a polite smile, stepped to the window with his interns and said a few words, which he accompanied with a perpendicular, swinging motion of his hand. After three minutes one of the young people, short-sighted and nervous, came back to the table and said, trying to look at me severely: "Do you sleep well, sir?" "No, badly." At which he jumped back again to the group. There the discussion went on for another while, then the doctor turned to me and informed me that I would be called. I reminded him that I had been told to come at one o'clock. He smiled and made a few quick, jerking motions with his small white hands, meant to say that he was uncommonly busy. So I went back to my corridor, in which the air had become much more stifling, and resumed walking up and down, although I was dead tired. Finally the damp, stuffy air made me dizzy; I stopped at the entrance door and opened it a little. I saw that outdoors it was still afternoon and there was still some sun; that was an inexpressible boon. But I had hardly been standing there a minute when I heard myself called. A woman sitting two steps away at a small table was hissing something at me. Who had told me to open the door. I could not stand the air, I replied. Good, that was my affair, but the door had to remain closed. Whether it might not be possible to open a window. No, that was forbidden. I decided to resume pacing up and down, because it was a kind of narcotic and bothered no one. But the woman at the small table now took a dislike to that too. Whether I didn't have a place to sit. No, I didn't. But walking around was not allowed; I would have to find a seat. There still must be one. The woman was right. There really was a place free beside the girl with the protruding eyes. There I sat, with the feeling that this state of affairs must without doubt be a preparation for something dreadful. To my left was this girl with the rotting gums; what was on my right I could only make out after a while. It was an enormous, motionless mass, which had a face and a big, heavy, motionless hand. The side of the face I saw was empty, completely without expressions and memories, and it was uncanny that his suit was like that of a corpse that had been dressed for the coffin. The narrow black tie was fastened around the collar in the same loose, impersonal fashion, and one could see from the coat that it had been put on this will-less body by others. The hand had been placed on these trousers where it lay, and even the hair was combed as if by the women who washed corpses, and was stiffly arranged like the hair of stuffed animals. I observed all this with attention, and it occurred to me that this was the place that had been destined for me, for I believed I had finally reached that place in my life at which I would remain. Yes, fate takes wondrous paths.

Suddenly, quite near to me, in quick succession, there arose the frightened, resisting cries of a child, followed by a soft, muffled weeping. While I strained to find out where that could have come from, there trembled again a small, suppressed cry, and I heard voices that were asking, a half-loud voice commanding, and then some sort of impersonal machine hummed, caring nothing for anything. Now I remembered the partial wall, and realized that all this came from beyond the doors, and that people were at work there. And indeed, from time to time the attendant in the soiled apron appeared and motioned. I no longer had any thought that he could mean me. Was it me? No. Two men came with a wheelchair; they lifted the mass into it, and now I saw that it was an old, paralyzed man who still had another, smaller, side worn down by life, with an open, dull, sad eye. They wheeled him in, and beside me there was lots of room. And I sat and wondered what they wanted to do with the imbecilic girl and whether she would cry out too. The machines in back were humming in such a pleasantly factory-like way, there was nothing worrisome about it.

But suddenly everything was silent, and into the silence a superior, self-satisfied voice that I thought I recognized said:

"*Riez!*" Pause. "*Riez. Mais riez, riez.*" I was already laughing. It was not clear why the man over there did not want to laugh. A machine started up clattering, but immediately stopped. Words were exchanged, then the same energetic voice rose, commanding: "*Dites-nous le mot: avant.*" Spelling: "*a-v-a-n-t*" . . . Silence. "*On n'entend rien. Encore une fois:* . . ."[8]

And then, while such warm and woolly babble came from the other side, for the first time in many, many years *it* was there again.

---

8 "Laugh! . . . laugh! . . . Say the word 'before' . . . I hear nothing. Once again."

That which had given me my first, profound horror when, as a child, I was in bed with a fever: the Big Thing. Yes, that's what I always said when everyone gathered around my bed and felt my pulse and asked what had frightened me: the Big Thing. And when they fetched the doctor and he came and spoke to me, I begged him to do everything to make the Big Thing go away, nothing else mattered. But he was like the others. He could not take it away, although at that time I was little and it would have been easy to help me. And now it was here again. Later it had simply stayed away, even in fevered nights it had not returned; but now it was here, although I had no fever. Now it was here. Now it grew out of me like a tumor, like a second head, and was part of me, although there was no way it could belong to me because it was so large. It was there like a big dead animal that once, when it was alive, had been my hand or my arm. And my blood went through me and through it as through one and the same body. And my heart had to strain hard to drive the blood into the great thing: there was almost not enough blood. And the blood entered the great thing unwillingly and came back ill and bad. But the great thing swelled and grew in front of my face like a warm bluish boil and grew in front of my mouth, and the shadow of its edge was already over my remaining eye.

I can not remember how I got out through all the courtyards. It was evening, and I got lost in the unfamiliar quarter and walked up boulevards with endless walls in one direction and then when there was no end back in the opposite direction to some square or other. From there I began to walk down a street and came to other streets that I had never seen, and still others. Overbright electric trolleys with hard, beating bells came rushing up and past. But on their placards were names I did not know. I did not know in what city I was and whether I had somewhere here a place to live and what I had to do in order not to have to walk any more.

And now on top of everything this illness that has always affected me so peculiarly. I am certain it is underestimated. Just as one exaggerates the significance of other illnesses. This illness does not have any specific characteristics, it adopts the characteristics of the person it attacks. With a sleepwalking sureness it plucks from each person his deepest danger, one that seemed past, and places it before him again, quite close, in the next hour. Men who once during their school years tried the helpless vice whose deceived lover was the poor, hard hands of boys find themselves at it again, or an illness they overcame as children starts up in them again; or an abandoned habit recurs, a certain hesitant turning of the head that they had had years before. And together with whatever recurs a whole tangle of wild memories arises that clings to it as wet seaweed clings to a sunken thing. Lives one would never have known about rise to the surface and mingle with what really was and repress past things one thought one knew: for in what rises up there is a new, rested energy, but what was always there is tired from being too often remembered.

I am lying in my bed, up five flights of stairs, and my day, which nothing interrupts, is like a dial without a hand. Like a thing long lost, that one morning is lying in its place, preserved and good, newer almost than when it was lost, just as if it had been in someone's care—thus here and there on my bedspread lost things from childhood are lying, and are like new. All the lost fears are here again.

The fear that a small wool thread sticking out from the hem of a blanket is hard, hard and sharp as a steel needle; the fear that this small button on my nightshirt is bigger than my head, big and heavy;

the fear that this crumb of bread now falling from my bed will hit the floor glassy and shattered, and the oppressive anxiety that everything would be broken along with it, everything, forever; the fear that along the edge of a letter that had been torn open there was something forbidden that no one should be allowed to see, something indescribably precious for which no place in my room was secure enough; the fear that if I fell asleep I would swallow the piece of charcoal lying in front of the stove; the fear that some number or other in my brain would begin to grow until it no longer had room in me; the fear that what I was lying on was granite, gray granite; the fear that I could scream and people would come running to my door and finally break it down, the fear that I could betray myself and give voice to everything I am afraid of, and the fear that I could not say anything, because everything is unsayable—and the other fears . . . the fears.

I have prayed for my childhood and it has come back, but I feel it is still just as heavy as it was then, and that it has been no use getting older.

Yesterday my fever was better, and today the day is beginning like spring, like the spring in paintings. I will try to go out, to the Bibliothèque Nationale to my poet, whom I have not read for so long, and perhaps later I can walk slowly through the gardens. Perhaps there is a breeze over the big pond that has such real water, and children will come to launch their boats with the red sails and watch them.

Today I didn't expect it, I went out so bravely, as if it were the simplest and most natural thing. But again there was something that seized me like paper, crumpled me up and threw me away, something incredible.

The Boulevard Saint-Michel was broad and empty, and it was easy walking along its gentle slope. Window shutters above opened with a glassy clatter, and their reflections flew over the street like a white bird. A wagon with bright red wheels came by, and further down someone was wearing something light green. Horses ran in shimmering harnesses on the dark, sprinkled pavement, which was clean. The wind was excited, new, mild, and everything rose up: odors, calls, bells.

I came past one of the cafés in which, in the evening, fake red gypsies play. The air of the night crept with a bad conscience from the open windows. Smoothly combed waiters were scrubbing in front of the door. One was bent over, throwing handful after handful of yellowish sand under the tables. One of the passersby nudged him and pointed down the street. The waiter, who was quite red in the face, looked sharply in that direction for a while, then a laugh spread over his beardless cheeks as if it had been spilled on them. He motioned to the other waiters, quickly turned his laughing face right and left a few times, to get everyone's attention and not to miss anything himself. Now they were all standing and looking down the street, searching, smiling or irritated because they had not yet discovered what there was to laugh about.

I felt a little fear beginning in me. Something was urging me to the other side of the street, but I only began to walk more quickly, involuntarily scrutinising the few people in front of me, about whom I noticed nothing remarkable. But I saw that one of them, a delivery boy in a blue smock carrying on one shoulder an empty basket with handles, was looking at someone. When he had had enough, he turned around on the same spot toward the buildings and made the rhythmic motion to his forehead that everyone knows to a laughing shop assistant across the street. Then he flashed his black eyes and came toward me swaying and satisfied.

I expected, as soon as my eye had room, to see some kind of unusual and striking figure, but I saw no one walking in front of me except a tall, gaunt man in a dark overcoat, with a soft black hat on his short, ash-blond hair. I assured myself that there was nothing ridiculous in this man's clothing or in his behavior, and was already trying to look down the boulevard past him when he stumbled over something. As I was close behind him I was careful, but when I came to the spot there was nothing there, absolutely nothing. We both went on, he and I, the distance between us remaining the same. Now we came to a crossing, and then it happened that the man in front of me hopped down the steps of the curb with uneven legs, something like the way children sometimes jump or hop up when they are walking and are happy. He went up the curb on the other side in one long stride. But hardly had he got up there when he drew in one leg a little and hopped on the other, once, and then quickly again and again. Now one might think this sudden motion was a stumbling, if one assumed that there had been a trifle there, a seed, the slippery skin of a fruit, anything; and the strange thing was that the man himself seemed to believe in the presence of some hindrance, for each time he looked at the offending spot with the half angry, half reproachful look people have at such moments. Once again a warning something called me to the other side of the street, but I paid no attention and continued on behind this man, concentrating my entire attention on his legs. I must confess that I felt remarkably relieved when for some twenty steps the hopping did not recur, but when I raised my eyes I noticed that the man had acquired another vexation. The collar of his overcoat had lifted up; and as he attempted with effort, now with one hand, now with both, to turn it down, he couldn't make it stay. That sort of thing happens. It did not worry me. But immediately afterward I noticed with boundless astonishment that there were *two* motions in this person's preoccupied hands: a secret, rapid one with which he imperceptibly flipped the collar up, and that other slower, explicit, as it were exaggeratedly spelled-out motion that was intended to pull the collar back down. This observation confused me so much that two minutes passed before I recognized that in this man's neck, behind the lifted collar and the nervously active hands, there was the same horrible, bi-syllabic hopping that had just left his legs. From this moment on I was bound to him. I understood that this hopping wandered around in his body, that it was attempting to break out here or there. I understood his fear of people, and I myself began to look carefully whether the passersby noticed anything. A cold shudder ran down my back when his legs suddenly made another small, jerking jump, but no one saw it, and I decided that I too would stumble a little, in case anyone noticed him. That would certainly have been a way of making curious people believe that there had only been some small, unobtrusive obstacle there that both of us had accidentally stepped on. But while I was thinking of helping out in this fashion, he himself had hit upon a new, excellent solution. I forgot to mention that he was carrying a cane. It was a simple cane of dark wood, with a plain round, curved handle. And in his groping fear he had hit upon the idea of holding this cane at his back, firmly against his spine, at first with one hand (for who knew what he might need the other for), shoving the round end of the cane into his coat collar so that one felt it hard and supportive behind the neck vertebrae and the first spinal vertebra. That was a posture that was not conspicuous, at most a little high-spirited; the unexpected spring day could account for it. It worked splendidly. To be sure, at the next crossing two hops burst out, two small, half-suppressed hops, quite unimportant; and the one really obvious hop was done so cleverly (just at that point a hose lay across the sidewalk) that there was nothing to be feared. Yes, it was still going well; from time to time his other hand also grasped the cane and pressed it more firmly, and the danger was again immediately overcome. Yet I could not do anything to keep my own fear from growing. I knew that, as he was walking and attempting with infinite effort to appear indifferent and distracted, the horrible twitching was building up in his body; the fear with which he felt it growing and growing was also in me, and I saw how he gripped the cane when the shaking inside him began. For the expression of his hands was so severe and unrelenting that I put all my hope in his will, which had to have been great. But what could will do here. The moment had to come when his strength was at an end, it could not be far off. And I, who was walking behind him with a strongly beating heart, I pulled together my little bit of energy like money, and as I looked at his hands begged him to please take it if he needed it.

I believe that he did take it; what could I do that it was not more.

There were many vehicles and people rushing to and fro on the Place Saint-Michel, we were often between two vehicles, and then he caught his breath and relaxed a little, as if to rest, and then there was a little hopping and a little nodding. Perhaps that was the trick with which the imprisoned illness was trying to overcome him. His will had been broken through in two places, and the yielding had left behind a gentle, enticing irritation in the possessed muscles, and the two compelling beats. But the cane was still in its place, and his hands looked stern and angry. In this way we started across the bridge, and it was going all right. It was all right. But now something irresolute came into his step, now he ran two steps, and now he stopped. His left hand gently released itself from the cane and raised itself up, so slowly that I saw it tremble in the air; he pushed his hat back a little and passed his hand over his forehead. He turned his head a little, and his glance swayed without seeing over sky, buildings, and water, and then he gave in. The cane was gone, he stretched out his arms as if he was about to fly away, and it broke out of him like a force of nature and bent him forward and tore him backward and made him nod and bow and hurled the power of dance out of him among the crowd. For many people were already around him, and I saw him no more.

What would have been the sense of going somewhere after that, I was empty. I drifted past the buildings up the boulevard again like an empty piece of paper.

I'm trying to write you,[9] although there is really nothing to say after a necessary parting. But I'm trying anyway, I think I must, because I have seen the saint in the Pantheon, the lonely, sainted woman and the ceiling and the door, and inside the lamp with its modest circle of light, and out there the sleeping city and the river and the distance in the moonlight. The saint watches over the sleeping city. I wept. I wept because it was all so suddenly, so unexpectedly *there*. I wept before it, I couldn't help myself.

I am in Paris, those who hear it are glad, most people envy me. They are right. It is a great city, large, full of remarkable temptations. For my part, I must admit that in a certain way I have given in to

---

9   Draft of a letter (Rilke's note).

them. I don't think it can be put any other way. I have yielded to these temptations, and that has brought about certain changes, if not in my character at least in my view of the world, in any case in my life. Under these influences a totally different conception of things has formed in me, certain differences have appeared that separate me from people more than anything that has gone before. A transformed world. A new life full of new meanings. At the moment it is rather hard for me, because everything is too new. I am a beginner in my own relationships.

Whether it might not be possible, once, to see the ocean?

Yes, but just think I was imagining that you could come. Would you perhaps have been able to tell me whether there is a doctor? I forgot to ask about it. Besides, I don't need that any more.

Do you remember Baudelaire's incredible poem "Une Charogne"?[10] It may be that now I understand it. Except for the last stanza, he was in the right. What was he to do, once he encountered that? It was his task to see in this horrible form that exists, repulsive only in appearance, its validity amidst all that exists. There can be no selecting out or rejecting. Do you think it an accident that Flaubert wrote his *Saint Julien l'Hospitalier*? It seems to me as if that was the decisive thing: whether one can summon up the strength to lie down beside the leper and warm him with the heat of the heart in nights of love; that can turn out no other way but well.

Please don't believe that I am suffering here from disappointments; on the contrary. I am sometimes surprised at how readily I give up everything that was expected in favor of the real, even when it is terrible.

---

10   "A Carcass."

My God, if it were possible to impart something of it. But *would* it exist then, *would* it exist? No, it *is* only at the price of isolation.

The existence of the horrible in every component of the air. You breathe it in transparently, but within you it condenses, grows hard, assumes pointed, geometric forms among the organs; for all the torture and horror that has happened in places of execution, in torture chambers, in madhouses, in operating rooms, under the arches of bridges in late autumn: all of it has a tenacious permanence, it exists in itself, and in its terrible reality jealously clings to everything that exists. People would like to be able to forget much of this; their sleep gently abrades such furrows in their brain, but dreams drive sleep away and retrace the images. And people wake up gasping for breath and allow the light of a candle to dissolve in the darkness, and drink the half-bright reassurance like sugared water. But alas, on what a fine edge this security balances. Just the slightest movement, and already the sight of known and friendly things vanishes, and it becomes clearer that the contour that was just now so comforting is the edge of horror. Beware the light that makes space more hollow; don't look around, lest a shadow rise like your master behind your sitting up. Better, perhaps, had you remained in darkness, and if your unconfined heart had sought to be the heavy heart of everything that could not be made out. Now you have gathered yourself together within yourself, you see yourself cease in your hands, from time to time with a vague motion you trace your face. But within you there is almost no space; and it nearly calms you that in this constriction within you it is impossible for something very great to find room; that the incredible too must come into being within, and adapt itself to the conditions it finds. But outside, out there, it is impossible to foresee; when it rises up out there it also fills itself up in you, not in the vessels that are partially under your control, or in the lethargy of your more composed organs; it increases in the capillaries, sucked upward through their pipes into the furthest reaches of your infinitely branched existence. There it emerges, there it exceeds you, rises higher than your breath, to which you flee upward as the last place that is you. O and where to then, then where to? Your heart drives you out of yourself, your heart is coming after you, and you are standing almost outside yourself and can no longer get back. You spurt out of yourself like a beetle one steps on, and your little bit of outer hardness and adaptation is meaningless.

O night without objects. O out impassive windows, O carefully closed doors; settings from olden times, taken on, credited, never completely understood. O stillness in the staircase, stillness from adjoining rooms, stillness high up on the ceiling. O mother: O you, the only one who fended off all this stillness from me in the days of childhood. Who takes the stillness upon herself, saying: don't be frightened, it's me. Who has the courage in the night to completely be this shelter for what is afraid, what is desperate from fear. You strike a light, and are already the noise. And you hold the light in front of you and say: It's me, don't be frightened. And you put it down, slowly, and there is no doubt: it is you, you are the light around the kind, familiar things that are there without any deeper meaning, good, simple, unambiguous. And if there is a rustling in the wall somewhere, or a step in the hall: you only smile, smile, smile transparently on a bright background at the anxious face that is searching you out as if you were by agreement one with the secret and privy to its every undertone and in accord with it. Is any power of earthly rule like yours? Look: kings lie and stare, and the teller of stories is not able to divert them. On the blissful breasts of their favorites horror creeps over them and makes them tremble and lose desire. But you come and keep what is monstrous behind you and are completely and wholly in front of it; not like a curtain, which it could lift here or there. No, as if you had rushed past it when you heard the cry that needed you. As if you had come far in advance of everything that may come, and had at your back only your hastening here, your eternal path, the flight of your love.

The mask-maker I pass by every day has two masks hanging outside beside his door. The face of the young drowned girl molded in the morgue because it was beautiful, because it was smiling, so deceptively smiling, as if it knew.[11] And hanging below it, his knowing face.[12] This hard knot of tightly puckered thinking. This relentless self-compression of music incessantly trying to dissolve as vapor. The countenance of one whose hearing a god has closed off so that there would be no sounds but his. So that he would not be misled by the muddiness and frailty of noises. He, within whom was their clarity and duration; so that only soundless sense would bring world into him, soundlessly, a tense, expectant world, unready, before the creation of the sound.

You who completed the world: the way that what falls as rain over the earth and on the waters falls heedlessly, falls indifferently, arises again out of everything, more invisible and happy following its law, rises and hovers and forms the sky; so from you rose the

---

11   A young girl who had drowned herself in the Seine, and whose death mask seized the popular imagination.

12   Beethoven's death mask.

ascent of our precipitations and enveloped the world in music. Your music: that it might be about the world, not about us. That a piano might have been built for you in Upper Egypt, and an angel would have led you before the lonely instrument, through the ranges of the desert mountains in which kings rest and hetaeras and anchorites. And the angel would have bounded upwards and away, fearful that you would begin.

And then you would have streamed, streaming one, unheard; giving back to the cosmos what only the cosmos can bear. The Bedouins would have raced by in the distance, superstitious; but the tradesmen would have thrown themselves down at the edge of your music, as if you were the storm. Only occasional lions would have circled far around you by night, frightened of themselves, threatened by their agitated blood.

For who can now retrieve you from lascivious ears? Who is it who drives them out of concert halls, those prostituted ones with sterile hearing that whores but never conceives? Seed spurts, and they hold themselves under it like streetwalkers and play with it, or it falls among them all like the seed of Onan as they lie there in their unachieved gratification.

But where, Master, might there be a virginal youth with unviolated ears to lie with your sound: he would die of bliss or deliver the infinite, and his fertilized brain would burst from pure birth.

I don't underestimate it. I know it takes courage. But let's assume for a moment that someone had it, this *courage de luxe*, to follow them, and then forever know (for who could forget it again or confuse it with something else?) where they creep to afterward and what they do during the slow rest of the day and whether they sleep at night.

That would be especially important to find out: whether they sleep. But courage alone won't do it. For they don't come and go like everyone else, to follow whom would be a trifle. They are here and gone again, put down and taken away like lead soldiers. One finds them in a few out-of-the-way places that are by no means hidden. The shrubbery recedes, the path turns a little around the grass plot: there they stand and have lots of transparent space around them, as if they were under a bell jar. You might take them for pensive strollers, these inconspicuous men of small, in every respect modest figure. But you are wrong. Do you see their left hand, how it gropes for something in the torn pocket of the old overcoat; how they find it and take it out and hold up the small object awkwardly and conspicuously in the air? Within a minute, two, three birds appear, sparrows, who hop up, curious. And if the man succeeds in matching their quite precise conception of immobility, there is no reason why they should not come still closer. Finally the first bird rises and flutters nervously for a while at the height of that hand, which (God knows) is holding out, with undemanding, expressly renouncing fingers, a small, worn piece of sweet roll. And the more people who gather around him, at a suitable distance of course, the less he has in common with them. He stands there like a candle that is burning out, shining with what remains of its wick, and it makes him quite warm, but he has not stirred. And the many small, stupid birds have no way of judging how he beckons, how he entices. If there were no spectators and one let him stand there long enough, I am certain that suddenly an angel would appear, and, overcoming its resistance, eat the stale sweetish morsels out of the wasted hand. For that to happen, people are in the way, now as always. They see to it that only birds come; they find that quite enough, and maintain that he is not expecting anything else for himself. What else should it expect, this old, rain-spotted puppet sticking slightly aslant in the earth like ships' figureheads in the little gardens at home; does its posture too come from having once stood somewhere like a figurehead in front of its life, where the motion is greatest? Is it now so faded because it was once so colorful? Will you ask it?

But don't ask the women, if you see one feeding the birds. You can even follow them; they do it in passing; it would be easy. But leave them. They don't know how it happened. They suddenly have a lot of bread in their bag, and they hold out big pieces from their thin mantillas, pieces slightly chewed and moist. It does them good that their saliva goes out a little into the world, that the small birds fly around with this bitter aftertaste, even if they of course immediately forget it again.

There I sat over your books, obstinate one,[13] and tried to construe them as the others do, who do not leave you whole but have taken their portion, satisfied. For I did not yet understand fame, this public demolition of something still forming, onto whose construction site the crowd breaks in, scattering its stones.

Young man somewhere, in whom something rises that makes him tremble, use it so that no one knows you. And if those who dismiss you contradict you, if those with whom you associate abandon you completely, and if they want to obliterate you to make off with your dear thoughts: what, against this clear danger that keeps you at one with yourself, is the later cunning animosity of fame, which renders you harmless by scattering you about.

---

13   Ibsen.

Ask no one to speak of you, not even contemptuously. And when time passes and you notice how your name is spreading around among people, don't take it more seriously than any of the other things you find on their lips. Think: your name has turned bad, and get rid of it. Take on another, any other, so that God can call you in the night. And conceal it from everyone.

You, most lonely, most remote: how they have appropriated you for your fame. How long ago was it that they were bitterly against you, and now they embrace you as one of their own. And they carry your words around with them in the cages of their darkness and trot them out in public squares and poke them a little from within their sense of security. All your terrible beasts of prey.

That was when I first read you, when the beasts broke free and fell upon me in my desert, the desperate ones. Desperate as you yourself were in the end, you whose course is falsely marked on all the maps. It goes through the sky like a crack, this hopeless hyperbole of your trajectory, that only once bends down to us and rushes away filled with horror. What did you care whether a wife stays or leaves, or whether this person is caught up in fraud or that one in madness, or whether the dead are alive and the living apparently dead; what did you care? That was all so natural for you; you walked through it as one walks through an antechamber, and you did not stop. But you tarried and bent down where our happening boils and precipitates and changes color, inwardly. More inward than where anyone had ever been; a door had sprung open for you, and you were now with the pistons in the fiery light. There where you never took anyone along, mistrustful one, there you sat and weighed transitions. And there, because expounding was in your blood, and not forming or saying, there you made the tremendous resolve to enlarge, all by yourself, this tiny speck that you yourself at first saw only through magnifying lenses, in such a way that it would appear gigantic to thousands, to everyone. Your theater came into being. You could not wait for this life that took up almost no space, which centuries had concentrated into drops, to be discovered by the other arts and slowly made visible for individuals who gradually come together in insight, and who finally demand collectively to see the illustrious rumors confirmed in the metaphor of the stage that is opened up before them. You could not wait for this, you were there, you had to do the barely measurable: a feeling that rose half a degree; the tiny variation of a will hardly burdened by anything, which you read from close up; the thin cloudiness in a drop of longing, and the invisible color change in an atom of confidence: this you had to ascertain and hold fast; for life was now in such processes, our life that had glided into us and withdrawn inside, so deep that there were still hardly any suppositions about it.

The way you, a timeless tragic poet, were intent on showing, you had to transform this capillary activity in a single stroke into the most convincing gestures, the most intensely present things. You struggled with the unparalleled violence of your work, that more and more impatiently, more and more desperately, sought among the visible equivalents for the inwardly seen. There was a rabbit, an attic, a hall in which someone paces up and down. There was the tinkle of glasses in the adjoining room, a fire outside the windows, there was the sun. There was a church and a rocky valley that was like a church. But that wasn't enough; finally towers had to be brought in and whole mountain ranges, and avalanches that bury landscapes: inundated stages overloaded with graspable things for the sake of the ungraspable. Then you could do no more. The two ends that you had bent together sprang apart; your insane energy escaped from the elastic rod, and your work was undone.

Who could otherwise understand that at the end you did not want to leave the window, obstinate as you always were. You wanted to see the passersby; for the thought came to you that perhaps one day one could make something of them, if one could resolve to begin.

At that time it first occurred to me that there was nothing one could say about a woman; I noticed how they left her out whenever they talked about her, how they named and described the others, the surroundings, the localities, the objects, up to a certain point where all that ceased, gently and as it were cautiously ceased with the casual, never retraced contour that enclosed them. What was she like? I asked then. "Blonde, about like you," they said, and toted up all sorts of other things they knew; but in doing so they were once again quite vague about her, and I could not form any kind of picture at all. Really *seeing* her was something I could only do when Mama told me the story that I always insisted on hearing.

Then, every time she came to the scene with the dog, she used to close her eyes and insisted on holding her face, completely tight-lipped but everywhere shining through, between her two hands, which touched her face coolly at the temples. "I saw it, Malte," she insisted, "I saw it." She was already in her last years when I heard her say this. At the time when she no longer wanted to see anyone, and when she always, even on trips, had with her the small, closely-woven silver strainer through which she passed every drink. She no longer ate solid food, except for some biscuit or bread that, when she was alone, she would break into pieces and eat crumb by crumb, the way children eat crumbs. By then her fear of needles dominated her completely. She just said to others, to excuse herself, "I can't eat anything at all any more, but please don't let it bother you, I am perfectly fine." But she could suddenly turn to me (for I was already somewhat grown up) and say with a smile that cost her great effort: "How many needles there are, Malte, and how they are lying around everywhere, and to think that they can fall out so easily . . ." She made an effort to say it quite jokingly; but she was shaken with horror at the thought of all the loosely fastened needles that could fall into her food at any moment.

But when she told about Ingeborg, then nothing could happen to her; then she did not spare herself; then she spoke more loudly, then she laughed remembering Ingeborg's laugh, then one might see how beautiful Ingeborg was. "She made us all happy," she said, "your father too, Malte, literally happy. But when we were told that she would die, although she seemed only a little ill, and we all went around hiding it, she suddenly sat up in bed and said to herself, like someone who wants to hear how something sounds, 'You mustn't be so solicitous; we all know it, and I can set your minds at rest, it is good the way it is happening, I don't want to go on any longer.' Imagine, she said: 'I don't want to go on any longer.' She, who made us all happy. Will you understand that when you are grown up, Malte? Think about it later, perhaps it will occur to you. It would be fine if there were someone who understands such things."

"Such things" preoccupied Mama when she was alone, and she was always alone those last years.

"I will never think of it, Malte," she sometimes said with her strangely bold smile that did not want to be seen by anyone but completely fulfilled its purpose by being smiled. "But that no one is bothered to find it out: if I were a man, yes, especially if I were a man, I would think about it properly, step by step and from the beginning. For there must be a beginning, and if one could get hold of it that would at least be something. Oh Malte, we just go on living, and it seems to me that everyone is distracted and busy and no one pays proper attention as we go along. As if a meteor were to fall and no one sees it and no one has made a wish. Never forget to wish for something, Malte. One should not give up wishing. I don't believe that there is any fulfillment, but there are wishes that last a long time, all one's life, so that one can't wait long enough for the fulfillment."

Mama had had Ingeborg's small desk brought up to her room. I often found her sitting at it, for I was allowed to go in without ceremony. My footsteps disappeared completely in the carpet, but she felt me and held out one of her hands to me over her shoulder. This hand was completely weightless, and kissing it was almost like kissing the ivory crucifix I was handed in the evening before I went to sleep. She was sitting as before a musical instrument at this low secretary, whose writing shelf opened before her. "There is so much sun in it," she said, and truly, the inside was remarkably bright, of old, yellowed lacquer on which flowers were painted, always a red one and a blue one. And where three stood alongside one another there was a violet one in between, separating the other two. These colors, and the green of the narrow, vertical vine tendrils had become just as darkened as the ground was radiant, without actually being clear. The result was a strangely muted relationship of tones that stood in inwardly reciprocal relationships without speaking about them.

Mama pulled out the small drawers, which were all empty.

"Ah, roses," she said, leaning forward a little into the dim smell that had not entirely vanished. She always had the notion when she did this that something might suddenly be found in a secret compartment that no one had thought of, that would only yield to the pressure of some kind of hidden spring. "Suddenly it will spring open, you'll see," she said gravely and anxiously, and pulled hastily on all the drawers. But she had carefully folded whatever papers had really been left in the compartments and locked them up without reading them. "I wouldn't understand it, Malte, it would certainly be too hard for me." She was convinced that everything was too complicated for her. "There are no classes in life for beginners, always what is hardest is demanded of you right away." I had been assured that she had got this way only after the terrible death of her sister, Countess Öllegaard Skeel, who burned to death before a ball as she was trying to arrange the flowers in her hair before a candle-lit mirror. But recently it was Ingeborg who seemed to her the most difficult to understand.

And now I will write down the story the way Mama told it when I begged her for it.

It was midsummer, on the Thursday after Ingeborg's funeral. Sitting on the terrace where tea was served, one could see between the giant elms the pediment of the family mausoleum. The table was set as if one person more had never sat there, and we were all sitting casually spread out around it. Everyone had brought something along, a book or a workbasket, so that we were even a little cramped. Abelone (Mama's youngest sister) poured the tea, and everyone was busy handing things around, only your grandfather was looking at the house from his armchair. It was the hour when the mail normally came, and it had usually been Ingeborg who brought it, as she stayed in the house longer seeing to the arrangements for dinner. During the weeks of her illness we had had plenty of time to get used to her not coming; for we knew she could not come. But on this afternoon, Malte, when she really could no longer come—she came.

Perhaps it was our fault; perhaps we called her. For I remember that I was suddenly sitting there and intent on trying to think what it really was that was different. It was suddenly not possible for me to say *what*; I had completely forgotten it. I looked up and saw all the others turned toward the house, not in any particular, noticeable way, but quite calmly and everyday in their expectation. And then I was about to—(I shiver, Malte, when I think about it) but, God preserve me, I was about to say, "Where can she be—" when Cavalier, as he always had, shot out from under the table and ran to meet her. I saw it, Malte, I saw it. He ran to meet her, although she had not come; for him she had. We understood that he was running to her. Twice he looked around at us, as if asking. Then he rushed up to her like always, Malte, just like always, and reached her; for he began to jump around, Malte, all around something that was not there, and then jumped up on her to lick her, jumped right up. We heard him whimper with joy, and as he sprang in the air, several times in quick succession, one might really have thought he was hiding her from us with his jumps. But suddenly there was a howl, and he twisted in midair and fell back with remarkable awkwardness, and lay there quite strangely flattened out and did not stir. From the opposite side the servant came out of the house with the letters. He hesitated for some time; it was obviously not easy to approach our faces. And your father motioned him to stay where he was. Your father, Malte, had no love for animals; but now he went over, slowly as it seemed to me, and bent over the dog. He said something to the servant, something short, monosyllabic. I saw how the servant rushed over to gather up Cavalier. But your father picked up the animal himself and took it, as if he knew exactly where, into the house.

Once, when it had grown almost dark during this story, I was close to telling Mama about the "hand": at that moment I would have been able to. I was already taking a deep breath to begin, but then it occurred to me how well I understood the servant for not having been able to approach their faces. And in spite of the darkness I was afraid of Mama's face if it were to see what I had seen. I took another breath, so it would look like that was all I wanted to do. Several years later, after the remarkable night in the gallery at Urnekloster, I devoted myself for days to trying to confide in little Erik. But after our nighttime conversation he had once again completely shut himself off from me, he avoided me; I believe he despised me. But just for that reason I wanted to tell him about the "hand." I imagined he would think better of me (and for some reason I ardently wished he would) if I could make him understand that it was something I really experienced. But Erik was so clever at avoiding me that it never happened. And we left soon after. So this is, strangely enough, the first time that I am telling (and ultimately, too, only to myself) an event that lies far back in my childhood.

I can tell how small I must have been then because I was kneeling on the chair so I could comfortably reach the table on which I was drawing. It was evening, in winter if I'm not mistaken, in our apartment in town. The table stood in my room, between the windows, and there was no other lamp in the room but the one shining on my paper and on Mademoiselle's book; for Mademoiselle was sitting beside and somewhat behind me, reading. She was far away when she read, I don't know whether she was in the book; she could read for hours, she seldom turned the pages, and I had the impression that the pages became fuller and fuller beneath her gaze, as if she were looking additional words into them, specific words that she needed and that were not there. That's how it seemed to me while I was drawing. I drew slowly, without any particular purpose, and looked it over, when I did not know how to proceed, with my head inclined a little to the right; that way I would always discover most quickly what was still missing. Officers on horses were riding into battle, or they were in the thick of it, and that was much easier because then you only needed to draw the smoke that covered everything. Mama, however, always insisted it was islands I was drawing, islands with big trees and a castle and stairs and flowers at the edges that was supposedly reflected in the water. But I believe she was making that up, or it must have been later.

It is certain that on that evening I was sketching a knight, a single, very clear knight on a horse with remarkable trappings. He took so many colors that I frequently had to change pencils, but above all I most often used the red one, which I reached for again and again. Now I needed it once more; it rolled (I can still see it) diagonally across the sheet in the lamp light at the edge of the table, and before I could prevent it fell past me and was gone. I really needed it urgently, and it was quite irritating to have to climb down after it. Awkward as I was, I had to negotiate all sorts of maneuvers to get down: my legs seemed much too long, I couldn't get them out from under me; the kneeling position I had been in too long had made my limbs numb, I didn't know what was part of me and what was part of the chair. But finally I did get down, somewhat confused, and found myself on an animal skin that reached under the table back to the wall. But then a new difficulty presented itself. Adjusted to the light up above and still all excited about the colors on the white paper, my eyes could not make out the slightest thing under the table, where the blackness seemed to me so tightly closed that I was afraid of bumping against it. So I relied on my sense of touch and, kneeling and supported on my left hand, combed through the cool, shaggy carpet that felt so good to the touch; except that no pencil was to be felt. I imagined I was losing a lot of time, and was about to call Mademoiselle and ask her to hold the lamp for me, when I noticed that the darkness was slowly becoming penetrable to my involuntarily straining eyes. I could already make out the wall in back, which ended at a bright baseboard. I oriented myself by the legs of the table; above all I recognized my own, outstretched hand moving around down below all by itself, a little like some aquatic animal investigating the bottom. I looked at my hand, I still remember, almost curiously; it seemed as if it could do things I had not taught it as it tapped around down there so independently, with motions I had never seen it make. I pursued it as it pressed forward, it interested me, I was prepared for anything. But how could I have been prepared for another hand suddenly coming out of the wall toward mine, a bigger, uncommonly skinny hand of a kind I had never seen. It was searching around in similar fashion from the other side, and both outstretched hands were blindly moving toward each other. My curiosity was still not all used up, but suddenly it was at an end, and only horror remained. I felt that one of the hands belonged to me and that it was letting itself in for something that was not to be made good again. With all the power that I had over it I stopped it and pulled it back, flat and slow, not taking my eyes off the other hand, which went on groping. I understood that it would not give up. I can't say how I got up again. I sat crouched down in the chair, my teeth were chattering, and I had so little blood in my face that it seemed to me there was no blue left in my eyes. I wanted to say "Mademoiselle" but couldn't, but she took fright herself, threw down her book and knelt beside my chair and called out my name; I think she shook me. But I was quite conscious. I swallowed a few times; for now I wanted to relate it.

But how? I pulled myself indescribably together, but it was not to be expressed in a way that anyone could understand it. If there were words for this event I was too small to find them. And suddenly I was seized by the fear that they could, beyond my age, suddenly be there, these words, and it seemed to me more terrible than anything to then have to utter them. To have to go through the reality down below once again, from the beginning, differently, modified; to hear myself admitting it. For that I no longer had any strength.

Of course it is imagination if I now maintain that already at that time I felt that something had come into my life, right into my life, which I would have to carry around alone, always and always. I see myself lying on my little cot and not sleeping, somehow vaguely fore-seeing that this is the way life would be: full of nothing but strange things that are intended for only *one person* and that cannot be said. What is certain is that gradually a mournful and heavy pride arose in me. I imagined how one would go around filled with inner things and be silent. I felt an impetuous sympathy for grown-ups; I admired them, and resolved to tell them that I admired them. I resolved to tell Mademoiselle at the first opportunity.

And then came one of those illnesses that seemed bent on proving to me that this was not the first private experience. Fever raged in me and dredged up from the depths experiences, images, and facts I had known nothing about. I lay there bombarded with myself, and waited for the moment when I would be ordered to put every-thing in me in its place again, properly, in sequence. I began, but it grew under my hands, it resisted, there was much too much. Then rage seized me, and I threw everything into myself in a heap and crammed it down; but I could not close myself again over it. And then I screamed, half-open as I was, I screamed and screamed. And when I began to look outside myself they had long been standing around my bed and were holding my hands, and there was a candle, and its big shadows moved behind them. And my father ordered me to say what the trouble was. It was a friendly, muted order, but still an order. And he became impatient when I didn't answer.

Mama never came at night—or yes, she came once. I had screamed and screamed, and Mademoiselle had come and Sieversen the housekeeper, and Georg the coachman; but it had been of no avail. They finally sent the coach for my parents, who were at a great ball, I think at the Crown Prince's. And suddenly I heard the coach coming into the courtyard and I was still, sat up, and looked toward the door. And then there was a little rustle in the other rooms and Mama came in wearing her great court dress, to which she paid no attention, and almost running let her white fur fall to the floor behind her and took me in her bare arms. And I, astonished and delighted as never before, ran my fingers over her hair and her small, well-groomed face and the cold jewels on her ears and the silk at the edge of her shoulders, which smelled of flowers. And we stayed like that, weeping and kissing tenderly, until we felt that Father was there and that we had to separate. "He has a high fever," I heard Mama say timidly, and Father reached for my hand and counted the pulse. He was wearing the Master of the Hunt's uniform with the beautiful broad blue watered-silk band of the Order of the Elephant. "What nonsense to call us," he said into the room, without looking at me. They had promised to return if it was nothing serious. And it was indeed nothing serious. But on my coverlet I found Mama's dance card and white camellias, which I had never seen and which I laid upon my eyes when I noticed how cool they were.

But what was long in such illnesses were the afternoons. Sleep always came in the morning after the bad night, and when one woke up and thought it was early again, it was afternoon and stayed afternoon and never ceased being afternoon. There one lay in the tidied-up bed and perhaps grew a little in the joints and was much too tired to think of anything. The taste of applesauce lasted a long time, and that already meant a great deal if one somehow involuntarily stretched it out and allowed the clean sourness to go around in one instead of thoughts. Later, when strength returned, the pillows were piled up at one's back and one could sit up and play with soldiers; but they fell down so easily on the shaky bed tray, and then the whole array all at once; and one was not so far restored to life as to be able to begin over and over again. Suddenly it got to be too much and one asked for everything to be quickly taken away, and it was good to see only my two hands again, a bit further down on the empty coverlet.

When Mama came for half an hour and read fairy tales (Sieversen was there for proper, long readings), it was not for the sake of the tales. For we were agreed that we did not like fairy tales. We had a different notion of the miraculous. We found that it was always most miraculous if everything happened by natural means. We didn't hold much with flying through the air, fairies disappointed us, and we expected only a very superficial change from transformations. But still we read a little in order to look busy; it bothered us, if someone came in, to have to explain what we happened to be doing. We were especially clear on this point with Father.

Only when we were quite certain not to be disturbed and it was twilight outside, it could happen that we gave ourselves over to memories, mutual memories, that seemed old to both of us and that we smiled over; for we had both grown up since. It occurred to us that there had been a time when Mama wanted me to be a little girl and not this boy that I actually was. I had somehow guessed this, and the idea came to me of sometimes knocking on Mama's door in the afternoon. When she asked who was there I was happy to call out "Sophie" from outside, making my little voice so dainty that it tickled my throat. And when I went in (in the small, girlish smock that I usually wore, with the sleeves completely rolled up) I was simply Sophie, Mama's little Sophie, who was busy about the house and who had to braid Mama's hair, so that there could be no confusion with bad Malte, if he should ever come back. His return was by no means desired: both Mama and Sophie found it pleasant that he was gone, and their conversations (which Sophie always continued in the same high voice) consisted mostly in counting up Malte's naughtinesses and complaining about him. "Ah yes, that Malte," Mama sighed. And Sophie knew in general a great deal about how bad boys were, as if she knew a whole crowd of boys.

"I would like to know what has happened to Sophie," Mama suddenly said in the course of our remembering. Malte could, of course, provide no information about that. But when Mama proposed that she surely must have died, he stubbornly contradicted her and implored her not to believe it, as little as it could be proved otherwise.

When I think about it now, I can wonder at how I managed again and again to come back entirely from the world of these fevers, to find myself in the thoroughly shared life in which everyone wanted be reinforced in the feeling of being among people one knew, and where one got along so cautiously in the world of common understanding. In that world something was expected, and it either came or it didn't, there was no third possibility. There were things that were sad, sad once and for all, there were pleasant things, and a whole host of incidental ones. But if a joy had been prepared for one it was a joy, and one had to act accordingly. Basically it was all quite simple, and once you had figured it out it happened as if of its own accord. Everything was fitted into these limits that were agreed upon: the long, unvarying school hours when it was summer outside; the walks about which one had to give a report in French; the visitors one was called in for and who found one droll, if one happened to be sad, and who made fun of one as of the dejected face of certain birds, that have no other. And of course the birthdays, on which one had to receive invited children one hardly knew, embarrassed children who made one embarrassed, or brazen ones who scratched one's face and broke what one had just gotten, and then suddenly went away when everything had been torn out of boxes and drawers and lay in heaps. But when one played alone, as usual, it could happen that without noticing it one stepped outside this agreed-upon and on the whole harmless world and found oneself in relationships that were entirely different and not at all foreseeable.

There were times when Mademoiselle had her migraines, which came on with uncommon severity, and those were the days on which I was hard to find. I know that if it occurred to Father to ask after me, the coachman was sent out into the grounds, but I was not there. I could look down from one of the guest rooms and see him running out and calling me at the beginning of one of the long walks. These guest rooms were located, one beside the other, in the attic of Ulsgaard and were, since at that time we seldom had houseguests, almost always empty. But next to them was the great corner room that had such a strong attraction for me. Nothing was to be found there but an old bust, which, I believe, represented Admiral Juel, but all around the room the walls were lined with deep, gray cabinets, in such a way that even the window had been inserted above them in the empty white wall. I had discovered the key in one of the cabinet doors, and it unlocked all the others. So in a short time I had investigated everything: the formal chamberlains' coats from the eighteenth century, quite cold from the inwoven silver threads, and the beautifully embroidered vests that went with them; the costumes of the Dannebrog and Elephant Orders, which one took at first for women's clothes, so rich and elaborate were they, and whose linings were so soft to the touch. Then real gowns that, filled out by their petticoats, hung stiffly like the puppets of a too-large play, so completely out of fashion that their heads had been put to other uses. But there were also cabinets in which it was dark when one opened them, dark with buttoned-up uniforms that looked much more used than everything else and that really desired not to be preserved.

No one will find it surprising that I took everything out and leaned into the light; that I held up this or that or put it around me; that I hastily pulled on a costume that more or less fit, and in it, curious and excited, ran into the nearest guest room, in front of the narrow pier mirrors made of individual, unevenly green pieces of glass. Ah, how one trembled to be in this mirror, and how enraptured when one was. When something approached from out of the cloudiness, more slowly than oneself, for the mirror did not, so to speak, believe it, and, sleepy as it was, did not want to repeat immediately what one had recited to it. Finally it had to, of course. But now it was something quite surprising, strange, quite different from what one had thought, something sudden, independent, that one quickly scanned but in the next moment had to recognize, not without a certain irony that could by a hair destroy the whole entertainment. But if one immediately began to speak, to bow, if one motioned to oneself, continually looking back at oneself, stepped back and then firmly and animatedly came forward again, then one had imagination on one's side, as long as one pleased.

That was when I learned the influence that can directly emanate from a particular costume. Hardly had I put on one of these outfits than I had to confess to myself that it had me in its power, that it dictated my motions, the expression on my face, indeed even my ideas; my hand, over which the lace sleeve kept falling, was not at all my usual hand; it moved like an actor, indeed I might say that it observed itself, as exaggerated as that sounds. These displacements, however, never went so far that I felt estranged from myself; on the contrary, the more variously I transformed myself the more convinced of myself I became. I grew bolder and bolder, I threw myself ever higher, for my skill at capturing was beyond all doubt. I did not notice the temptation in this rapidly growing sureness. All that was lacking for my undoing was that one day the last cabinet, which I had previously thought I could not open, yielded, providing me instead of particular costumes with all sorts of imaginative disguises whose fantastic approximations drove the blood into my cheeks. There was no counting all the things that were there. Besides a Venetian carnival mask that I recall, there were dominos in various colors, there were women's skirts that tinkled brightly with the coins sewn onto them, pierrots that I thought silly, and pleated Turkish pants and Persian caps from which little bags of camphor slipped out, and tiaras with stupid, expressionless stones. I despised all this a little; it was of such shabby unreality and hung there so flayed, so pathetic, shuffling together willlessly when one pulled it out into the light. But what intoxicated me were the roomy cloaks, the scarves, the shawls, the veils, all these large, yielding, unused materials that were soft and blandishing, or so smooth one could hardly grasp them, or so light that they flew past one like a breeze, or simply heavy with their whole burden. In them I saw for the first time really free and infinitely variable possibilities: of being a female slave who is sold, or Joan of Arc, or an old king or a magician; now one had all that in one's hand, especially since there were masks there too, large menacing or astonished faces with real beards and bushy or raised eyebrows. I had never seen masks before, but I immediately realized that masks had to be. I had to laugh when it occurred to me that we had a dog who looked as if he wore one. I thought of his warm eyes, that always looked out as if from behind into his shaggy face. I was still laughing as I dressed up, and it made me completely forget what it was that I wanted to pretend to be. Well, it would be new and exciting to decide that afterwards, in front of the mirror. The face that I tied on smelled peculiarly hollow, it firmly covered mine but I could comfortably look through it, and it was only after I had put on the mask that I chose all sorts of scarves, which I wound around my head in a sort of turban so that the edge of the mask, which disappeared below into a gigantic yellow cloak, was also almost entirely covered above and on the sides. Finally, when I could do no more, I considered myself sufficiently disguised. I grabbed a large staff that I paraded beside me at arm's length, and so, not without effort but, as it seemed to me, with great dignity, I dragged myself into the guest room and up to the mirror.

It was truly magnificent, it exceeded all expectations. And the mirror gave it back instantaneously, it was too convincing. It would not have been at all necessary to move much; this phenomenon was perfect even doing nothing. But it was important to find out what I really was, and so I turned a little and finally raised both arms, in large, as it were conjuring motions; that was, as I already noticed, the only right thing. But just at this solemn moment I heard quite nearby, muffled by my disguise, a complicated, composite noise. Quite frightened, I lost the being opposite me from view and was extremely vexed to perceive that I had upset a small round table holding God knows what kind of objects, apparently fragile. I bent down as well as I could and found my worst expectations confirmed: it looked as if everything was broken. The two superfluous, green-violet porcelain parrots were, of course, each in a different malicious manner, smashed to pieces. A jar, from which bonbons that looked like insects wrapped in silk cocoons rolled out, had cast its lid far away, one only saw half of it, the other half had completely disappeared. But most annoying was a flacon that had shattered into a thousand tiny fragments from which the remains of some sort of old perfume had spilled out that formed a spot of most repulsive physiognomy on the clear parquet. I quickly sponged it up with something or other that was hanging down on me, but the spot only became blacker and more unpleasant. I was at my wit's end. I got up and looked for some object with which I could put everything to rights. But none was to be found. Also, I was so hobbled in seeing and in every movement that rage rose within me against my ridiculous state, which I no longer understood. I pulled at everything, but it only clung more tightly. The lacing of the cloak strangled me, and the things on my head pressed down as if more and more were being piled on top. And the air had become clouded and as if misted up with the oldish vapor of the spilled liquid.

Hot and angry, I rushed to the mirror, and with effort looked through the mask at how my hands were agitating. But for this the mirror had just been waiting. The moment had come for it to get even. While I was straining with immeasurably growing apprehension to somehow extricate myself from my disguise, the mirror forced me, I don't know by what means, to look up, and dictated to me an image, no, a reality, an alien, incomprehensible monstrous reality with which I was saturated against my will: for now it was the stronger, and I was the mirror. I stared at this large, horrible unknown person before me, and it seemed to me uncanny to be alone with him. But in the very moment I was thinking this, the most extreme thing happened: I lost my senses, I simply broke down. For the length of a second I had an indescribable, grieving, and vain longing for myself, then there was only He: there was nothing but Him.

I ran away, but now it was He who ran. He knocked against everything, He didn't know the house, He didn't know where He was going; He got down a staircase, in a corridor He fell against a person who freed herself, screaming. A door opened, several people came out; oh, oh, how good it was to know them. It was Sieversen, the good Sieversen, and the maid, and the servant responsible for the silver: now it would be resolved. But they did not jump in and save me; their cruelty knew no bounds. They stood there and laughed, my God, they could stand there and laugh. I was weeping, but the mask wouldn't let the tears out, they ran over my face inside and instantly dried and ran again and dried. And finally I knelt down before them as no man has ever knelt; I knelt and raised up my hands to them and begged: "Get me out, if it can still be done, and save," but they did not hear; I no longer had a voice.

Till her dying day Sieversen told how I had sunk down and how they had gone on laughing, thinking that that was part of it. They were so accustomed to this from me. But I just lay there and didn't respond. And the horror, when they finally discovered that I was unconscious and lying there like a rag among all the cloths, nothing but a rag.

Time passed with incredible speed, and suddenly it was already so far along that it was time for the preacher, Dr. Jespersen, to be invited. It was for all concerned a laborious and protracted breakfast. Accustomed to the quite pious society in the neighborhood, which melted every time in his presence, with us he was distinctly out of place; he lay, so to speak, on land gasping for breath. The breathing through the gills that he had developed proceeded arduously, forming bubbles, and the whole thing was not without peril. Subject of conversation there was, if one wants to be precise, none at all; leftovers were disposed of at incredible prices, it was a liquidation sale of every inventory. With us Dr. Jespersen had to limit himself to being a private person; but that was precisely what he had never been. As far back as he could think, he had been employed in the soul department. The soul was for him a public institution that he represented, and he managed to arrange things so that he was never out of service, not even in dealing with his wife, "his modest, faithful Rebecca, who becomes blessed through childbearing," as Lavater expressed himself in another instance.

(As far as my father was concerned, his attitude toward God was perfectly correct and of immaculate politeness. In church it sometimes seemed to me that he was God's Master of the Hunt when he stood there patiently and bowed. It seemed to Mama, on the other hand, almost insulting that someone could be in a polite relation to God. It would have been a blessing for her if she could have come across a religion with clear and detailed rituals, kneeling for hours and casting herself down and acting properly with the large cross in front of her breast and gesturing with it around her shoulders.

She did not really teach me to pray, but it was reassuring to her that I liked to kneel and fold my hands, sometimes together and sometimes upright, whichever seemed to me at the time more expressive. Pretty much left to myself, I early on evolved through a series of stages that I only much later, in a period of despair, connected to God, but with such violence that He formed and shattered almost in the same instant. It is clear that after that I had to begin from the very beginning. And for this beginning I sometimes thought I needed Mama, although of course it was more proper to do it alone. But anyway, by then she had long been dead.)[14]

Toward Dr. Jespersen Mama could be almost exuberant. She entered into conversations with him that he took seriously, and when he heard himself speak she thought that that was enough and suddenly forgot him, as if he had already left. "How can he," she sometimes said of him, "travel around and go in to visit people when they are actually dying."

On that occasion he also came to her, but she certainly no longer saw him. Her senses failed, one after the other, her face first. It was in autumn, already time to move to the city, but that was just when she took sick, or rather, she immediately began to die, dying away slowly and miserably over her whole surface. The doctors came, and on a particular day they were all there together, taking over the whole house. For a few hours it was as if it belonged to the Privy Councilor and his assistants, and as if we had no further say in the matter. But immediately afterward they lost all interest, only came separately, as if from mere politeness, to accept a cigar and a glass of port. And meanwhile Mama died.

We were still waiting for Mama's only brother, Count Christian

---

14 Written in the margin of the manuscript (Rilke's note).

Brahe, who, as one will remember, had been serving for a time with the Turkish army, where, as it was always said, he had been highly decorated. He arrived one morning accompanied by an exotic servant, and I was surprised to see that he was taller than father, and apparently older, too. The two men immediately exchanged a few words which, as I surmised, concerned Mama. There was a pause. Then my father said, "She is quite disfigured." I didn't understand this expression, but shivered when I heard it. I had the impression as if my father too had to get hold of himself before he uttered it. But it was probably above all his pride that suffered in admitting it.

It was only several years afterward that I again heard Count Christian mentioned. It was at Urnekloster, and it was Mathilde Brahe who was fond of speaking of him. I am in the meantime certain that she exaggerated the individual episodes pretty high-handedly, for my uncle's life, about which only rumors reached the public and even the family, rumors that he never contradicted, could be interpreted in almost endless ways. Urnekloster is now in his possession. But no one knows whether he lives there. Perhaps he is still traveling, as was his habit; perhaps news of his death is on the way from some far distant corner of the globe, written in bad English by the hand of the exotic servant, or in some unknown language. Perhaps too this servant will give no sign of himself if he one day remains behind alone. Perhaps they have both long ago disappeared, and only appear on the passenger manifest of some lost ship under names that were not theirs.

Of course, if in those days at Urnekloster a coach drove up, I always expected to see *him* come in, and my heart beat in a strange way. Mathilde Brahe maintained: that's the way he would come, that would be his eccentricity, to suddenly be there when he was least expected. He never did come, but my power of imagination busied itself with him for weeks, I had the feeling that we owed it to each other to have a connection, and I would have gladly known something of him.

However, when soon thereafter my interests changed and, as the result of certain events, became wholly focused on Christine Brahe, I made no effort, strangely enough, to find out anything about the conditions of her life. On the other hand, the thought about whether her portrait was in the gallery worried me. And the desire to find out increased so obsessively and tormentingly that for several nights I did not sleep, until, quite unexpectedly, the night came in which I got up and went out with my candle, which seemed afraid.

As for myself, I was not thinking of fear. I was not thinking at all; I went. The high doors yielded so playfully before and above me, the rooms I went through remained quiet. And finally I noticed by the depth blowing toward me that I had entered the gallery. On the right I felt the windows with the night, and the pictures had to be on the left. I raised my candle as high as I could. Yes, there were the pictures.

First I undertook to look only at the women, but then I recognized one and another similar to those hanging at Ulsgaard, and when I illuminated them from below they stirred and tried to reach the light, and it seemed to me heartless not at least to wait for that to happen. There was, again and again, Christian the Fourth with the lovely woven side tress framing his broad, slowly curving cheeks. There were presumably his wives, of whom I only knew Kirstine Munk; and suddenly Frau Ellen Marsvin was looking out at me suspiciously in her widow's dress and with the same string of pearls on the brim of her high hat. There were King Christian's children: always new ones from new wives, the "incomparable" Eleonore on a white pony in her most splendid period, before her affliction. The Gyldenløves: Hans Ulrik, who the women in Spain thought painted his face, so filled with blood was he, and Ulrik Christian, whom one did not forget again. And almost all the Ulfelds. And that one, with one eye painted over black, might well be Henrik Holck, who was Imperial Count and Field Marshal at thirty-three, and this is how it happened: On the way to the demoiselle Hilleborg Krafse he dreamt that he would be given a bared sword instead of a bride. He took it to heart and turned around and began his short, audacious life that ended with the plague. I knew them all. We also had at Ulsgaard the ambassadors from the Congress of Nimwegen, who resembled each other a little because they had all been painted at the same time, each with the thin trimmed mustache outlining the sensual, almost gazing mouth. That I recognized Duke Ulrich was a matter of course, and Otte Brahe and Claus Daa and Sten Rosensparre, the last of his race; for I had seen paintings of them in the hall at Ulsgaard, or found engravings depicting them in old folders.

But there were many here whom I had never seen; not many women, but there were children. My arm had long since got tired and was trembling, but I raised the light again and again to see the children. I understood them, these little girls who were carrying a bird on their hand but had forgotten it. Sometimes a small dog was sitting below with them, a ball was lying there, and on the table by their side fruits and flowers; and in back there hung on a column, small and provisional, the coat of arms of the Grubbes or the Billes or the Rosenkrantzes. So many things had been gathered around them, as if there was a great deal to make amends for. But they were simply standing in their clothes and waiting; one saw that they were waiting. And then I had to think again of the women and of Christine Brahe, and whether I would recognize her.

I was about to run quickly to the end and walk back from there to look for her, but suddenly I ran into something. I turned around so violently that little Erik jumped back and whispered: "Watch out with that candle!"

"You here?" I said, breathless, and was not clear whether it was good or absolutely bad. He only laughed, and I didn't know what to do. My candle flickered, and I could not quite make out the expression on his face. It was probably bad that he was there. But then he said, coming closer, "*Her* portrait is not here, we are still looking for it upstairs." His low voice and his one moveable eye somehow pointed upward. And I understood that he meant the attic. But suddenly a remarkable thought came to me.

"We?" I asked. "So she is upstairs?"

"Yes," he nodded, standing close beside me.

"She herself is looking too?"

"Yes, we are looking."

"So it was put away, the picture?"

"Yes, imagine," he said, indignant. But I didn't quite understand what she wanted with it.

"She wants to see herself," he whispered, quite close.

"I see," I said, pretending that I understood. Then he blew out my candle. I saw how he leaned forward into the brightness, with his eyebrows arched high. Then it was dark. I involuntarily stepped back.

"What are you doing?" I called out in a strangled voice, and my throat was quite dry. He jumped after me and hung on my arm and giggled.

"Hey!" I yelled at him and tried to shake him off, but he hung on firmly. I couldn't keep him from putting his arm around my neck.

"Shall I say it?" he hissed, and a little saliva sprayed on my ear.

"Yes, yes, hurry up."

I didn't know what I was saying. Now he embraced me fully, stretching up.

"I have brought her a mirror," he said, and giggled again.

"A mirror?"

"Yes, because the portrait isn't here."

"No, no," I said.

He suddenly pulled me somewhat closer toward the window and pinched my upper arm so hard that I cried out.

"But she isn't in it," he blew into my ear.

Abruptly I pushed him away. Something snapped in him, I thought I had broken him.

"Oh come on," and now I had to laugh myself. "Not in it? How so, not in it?"

"You're stupid," he responded maliciously, no longer whispering. His voice had changed, as if he were now beginning a new, untried role. "One is either in it," he intoned severely and precociously, "then one is not here; or if one is here, one can't be in it."

"Of course," I answered quickly, without thinking. I was afraid that otherwise he would go away and leave me alone. I even reached out for him.

"Shall we be friends?" I proposed. He let himself be asked. "I don't care," he said impertinently.

I tried to begin our friendship, but didn't dare embrace him. "Dear Erik" was all I brought out, and touched him lightly somewhere. Suddenly I was very tired. I looked around; I no longer understood how I had got here and that I had not been afraid. I wasn't quite sure where the windows were, or the pictures. And as we left, he had to lead me.

"They won't do anything to you," he assured me magnanimously and giggled again.

Dear, dear Erik; perhaps you have been my only friend after all. For I have never had one. It's a pity that friendship meant nothing to you. There is so much I would have liked to tell you. Perhaps we would have got along. One can't know. I remember that your portrait was painted at that time. Grandfather had had someone come who painted you. An hour every morning. I can't recall what the painter looked like, I've forgotten his name, although Mathilde Brahe repeated it all the time.

Did he see you the way I see you? You were wearing a suit of heliotrope-colored velvet. Mathilde Brahe was in raptures over this suit. But that doesn't matter now. Only whether he saw you, that's what I would like to know. Let's assume it was a real painter. Let's assume he wasn't thinking that you could die before he was finished; that he did not look on the matter sentimentally at all; that he simply worked. That the asymmetry of your two brown eyes delighted him; that the motionless eye did not shame him in the least; that he had the tact not to put anything on the table beside your hand, with which you were perhaps steadying yourself a little; let's assume whatever else is necessary and grant it validity: a portrait is there, your portrait, in the gallery at Urnekloster, the last one.

(And if one walks along the gallery and has seen them all, there is yet one more boy there. One moment: who is it? A Brahe. Do you see the silver stake on the black ground and the peacock feathers? There's the name, too: Erik Brahe. Was that not an Erik Brahe who was executed? Of course, that's pretty well known. But this can't be the one. This boy died as a boy, doesn't matter when. Can't you see that?)

When we had visitors and Erik was called, Mathilde Brahe insisted every time that it was absolutely incredible how much he resembled old Countess Brahe, my grandmother. She was said to have been a great lady. I did not know her. On the other hand, I remember my father's mother very well, the real mistress of Ulsgaard. Mistress she always remained, however much she resented Mama for having come into the house as the bride of the Master of the Hunt. After that she constantly acted as though she had withdrawn, and sent the servants in to Mama with every trifle, while in important matters she made the decisions and dispositions calmly, without having to answer to anyone. Mama, I believe, did not want it otherwise. She was so little fashioned to supervise a great house, she completely lacked the ability to separate the important things from the incidental. Everything one said to her always seemed to her the whole of the matter, and it made her forget the rest that was also involved. She never complained about her difficulties. And to whom should she have complained? Father was an extremely respectful son, and grandfather had little to say.

Frau Margarete Brigge had always been, as far as I can remember, a tall, inaccessible old woman. I can't imagine it otherwise than that she must have been much older than the Chamberlain. She lived her life in our midst, without showing consideration for anyone. She was not dependent on any of us, and always had a sort of companion around her, an aging Countess Oxe, whom she had totally obligated to her through some charitable act. This must have been a unique exception, because charity was not otherwise her style. She didn't love children, and animals were not allowed in her vicinity. I don't know whether she loved anything else. It was said that as a very young girl she had been engaged to the handsome Felix Lichnowski, who then so horribly lost his life in Frankfurt. And indeed, after her death a portrait of the Prince was found that, if I am not mistaken, was returned to his family. Perhaps, I think to myself now, in this withdrawn country life that from year to year life at Ulsgaard had more and more become, she missed another, more brilliant life that would have been natural for her. It is hard to say if she regretted it. Perhaps she despised it because that life had not happened, because it had missed its opportunity to be lived with skill and talent. She had taken all this so far within herself and laid over it many brittle, shining, slightly metallic layers, of which whatever one happened to be on top looked cool and new. From time to time, to be sure, she betrayed herself through a naïve impatience at not receiving sufficient attention. In my time she could at table suddenly swallow the wrong way in some kind of obvious and complicated fashion that assured her of everyone's concern and let her appear, for a moment at least, as sensational and exciting as she might have wished to be in the great world. However, I suspect that my father was the only person who took these far too frequent incidents seriously. Politely bent forward, he looked at her, one could notice, as if in his thoughts he was, so to speak, placing his own properly functioning windpipe entirely at her disposal. The Chamberlain had of course likewise stopped eating; he took a small swallow of wine and refrained from offering any opinion.

He had stood up to his wife on just one occasion at table. It had been long ago, but the story was handed down maliciously and secretly; almost everywhere there was someone who had not yet heard it. The story was that at a certain time the Chamberlain's wife could get quite upset about wine stains spilled on the tablecloth through clumsiness; that she noticed such a stain, however it might have happened, and exposed it, so to speak, with the sharpest criticism. Once this had happened before several prominent guests. A few innocent stains, which she exaggerated, became the object of her scornful accusations, and however hard Grandfather tried through small signs and jocular remarks to dissuade her, she stubbornly stuck to her reproaches, which, however, she was forced to break off in the middle of a sentence. Something completely incomprehensible happened that had never occurred before. Grandfather had taken the bottle of red wine that was just then being passed around, and was engaged with the greatest attention in filling his glass himself. Except that, astonishingly, he did not stop pouring when the glass had long been full, but in the increasing silence slowly and carefully went on pouring, until Mama, who could never stop herself, laughed, and through her laughter made the entire incident harmless. For now everyone, relieved, joined in, and the Chamberlain looked up and handed the bottle to the servant.

Later another peculiarity gained the upper hand with my grandmother. She could not bear anyone in the house getting sick. Once, when the cook had hurt herself and she happened to see her with her bandaged hand, she maintained she could smell iodoform in the whole house, and it was hard to convince her that the person should not be dismissed. She did not want to be reminded of being sick. If someone was incautious enough to express before her some minor complaint, it was for her nothing other than a personal insult, and she long held it against the person.

The autumn Mama died, the Chamberlain's wife closed herself up in her rooms with Sophie Oxe and broke off all contact with us. Not even her son was admitted. It is true, this dying came most inopportunely. The rooms were cold, the stoves smoked, and mice had gotten into the house; one was nowhere safe from them. But that wasn't the only thing: Frau Margarete Brigge was indignant that Mama was dying; that something was on the agenda that she refused to speak about; that the young woman had the temerity to take this step before her, she who thought to die at some not yet determined time. For that she would have to die was something she thought about often. But she did not want to be rushed. She would die, of course, but when it pleased her, and then they could all die afterward if they were in such a hurry.

She never entirely forgave us for Mama's death. Moreover, she aged rapidly during the following winter. She still walked upright, but in a chair she collapsed, and she became harder of hearing. One could sit and stare at her wide-eyed for hours, she did not feel it. She was somewhere within; it was only seldom and for moments that she occupied her senses, which were empty, which she no longer inhabited. Then she said something to the Countess, who straightened her mantilla, and with her large, freshly washed hands she pulled her dress around her as if water had been spilled on it or as if we were not entirely clean.

She died one night toward spring, in town. Sophie Oxe, whose door stood open, had heard nothing. When they found her in the morning she was cold as glass.

Immediately afterward the Chamberlain's great and horrible illness began. It was as if he had been waiting for her end in order to die as inconsiderately as he had to.

It was in the year after Mama's death that I first noticed Abelone. Abelone was always there. That was for her a great disadvantage. And then Abelone was disagreeable, as I had established on some much earlier occasion, and I had never come to seriously revise my opinion. To ask what Abelone was really like would up to then have seemed to me almost ridiculous. Abelone was there, and one wore her out however one could. But suddenly I asked myself: Why was Abelone there? Each one among us had a definite sense of being there, even if it was not always as obvious as, for instance, the usefulness of Fräulein Oxe. But why was Abelone there? For a while it was said so that she could amuse herself. But that was forgotten. No one did anything to amuse Abelone. It did not seem in the least as if she were amusing herself.

Moreover there was one good thing about Abelone: she sang. That is, there were times when she sang. There was a strong, unwavering music in her. If it is true that angels are masculine, one might well say that there was something masculine in her voice: a radiant, heavenly masculinity. I, who even as a child had been so mistrustful of music (not because it lifted me out of myself more strongly than anything, but because I had noticed that it did not put me down at the place where it had found me, but deeper, somewhere completely in the unfinished), I could bear this music, on which one could rise upwards standing, higher and higher, until one thought, for a while, this must already have been heaven, more or less. I did not suspect that Abelone was to open still other heavens for me.

At first our relationship consisted in her telling me about Mama's girlhood. It was important for her to convince me how young and courageous Mama had been. At that time there was no one, she assured me, who was her equal in dancing or riding. "She was the boldest and tireless, and then suddenly she got married," Abelone said, still astonished after so many years. "It happened so unexpectedly, no one could understand it."

I was interested in why Abelone had not married. She seemed relatively old to me, and that she still could have married was something that did not occur to me.

"There was no one there," she answered simply, becoming truly beautiful. Is Abelone beautiful? I asked myself, surprised. Then I left home, went to the academy for the nobility, and an unpleasant and repugnant time began. But there at Sorö, when I stood apart from the others at the window and they left me in peace a little, I looked out into the trees, and in such moments and at night the certainty grew in me that Abelone was beautiful. And I began writing her all those letters, long and short, many secret letters in which I thought I was dealing with Ulsgaard and with my unhappiness. But they will have been, as I now see it, love letters. For finally it was vacation time, that at first had not wanted to come at all, and then it was as if by agreement that we did not meet in front of the others.

It had definitely not been arranged between us, but as the coach turned into the grounds I could not help getting out, perhaps only because I did not want to come driving up like some stranger. It was already high summer. I ran on one of the paths and toward a laburnum. And there was Abelone. Beautiful, beautiful Abelone.

I will never forget how it was when you looked at me. How you bore your looking, holding it up on your backward-inclining face as if, so to speak, it were something not fastened down.

Ah, whether the climate has not changed at all? Whether it has not become milder around Ulsgaard from all our warmth? Whether individual roses don't bloom longer now on the grounds, into December?

I will tell nothing about you, Abelone. Not because we deceived one another because even then you loved someone else, whom you have never forgotten, loving one, and I loved all women; but because the telling only gives rise to injustice.

There are tapestries here, Abelone.[15] I imagine that you are here, there are six tapestries, come, let us slowly stroll past them. But first step back and look at them all at once. How peaceful they are, aren't they? There is little variation in them. There is always this oval blue island hovering on a muted red ground full of flowers and inhabited by small animals occupied with themselves. Only there, in the last tapestry, the island rises up a little, as if it had become lighter. The island always bears a figure, a woman in various costumes, but she is always the same. At times there is a smaller figure beside her, a maidservant, and animals; the large ones, bearing coats of arms, are always part of the action. To the left a lion, and to the right, bright, the unicorn: they hold high above them the same banners that show three silver moons, rising, in a blue band on a red field.—Have you looked, will you begin with the first?

She is feeding the falcon. How magnificent her costume is. The bird is on her gloved hand and is stirring. She looks at it and reaches into the bowl that the maidservant is bringing her to offer it something. Below to the right, on the train of her dress, there is a small, silken-haired dog, looking up and hoping it will be remembered. And, have you noticed, the island is closed off in back by a low fence covered with roses. The coat-of-arms animals rise up in heraldic arrogance. They are wearing the shield, again, as a cloak. A beautiful clasp holds it closed. There is a breeze.

Does not one involuntarily walk more softly over to the next

---

15 In the Musée de Cluny, Paris.

tapestry, as soon as one perceives how lost in thought she is? She is weaving a wreath, a small, round crown of flowers. Pensively she chooses the color of the next carnation from the shallow basin the maidservant is holding out to her, as she winds the previous flowers together. Behind, on a bench, unused, stands a basket full of roses that has been discovered by a monkey. This time it is to be carnations. The lion is no longer interested, but on the right the unicorn understands.

Would not music have to come into this stillness, was it not already there, subdued? Heavily and silently adorned, she has stepped (how slowly, hasn't she?) to the portable organ and plays, standing, separated by the pipes from the maidservant, who is working the bellows on the other side. She has never been so beautiful. Her hair, woven in two braids, is strangely brought forward and joined together over her headpiece, so that the two ends, intertwined, stand up like the short plume of a helmet. Disgruntled, the lion endures the sounds, unhappily, suppressing its roar. But the unicorn is beautiful, undulating as in waves.

The island broadens out. A tent is set up. Of blue damask and flamed with gold. The animals raise it up and she advances, almost plain in her princely dress. For what are her pearls compared with herself. The maidservant has opened a small chest, and the lady is now lifting out a chain, a heavy, magnificent treasure that had always been locked away. The small dog is sitting beside her, raised on a place prepared for it, and is looking on. And have you discovered the motto up there on the tent? There stands: "A mon seul désir."[16]

What has happened, why is the little rabbit down below jumping

---

16   To my sole desire.

up, why does one see right away that it is jumping? Everything is so awkward. The lion has nothing to do. The lady herself is holding the banner. Or is she steadying herself on it? With her other hand she has grasped the horn of the unicorn. Is that grief, can grief be so upright and a mourning dress as discreet as this green-black velvet with the faded places?

But there is another festival, no one is invited to it. Expectation plays no role in it. Everything is there. Everything for always. The lion looks around almost threateningly: no one is allowed to come. We have never seen her fatigued; is she fatigued? Or has she only sat down because she is holding something heavy? One might think, a monstrance. But she inclines her other arm toward the unicorn, and the animal arches its back with pleasure and rears up and supports itself on her lap. What she is holding is a mirror. You see: she is showing the unicorn its image.

Abelone, I imagine that you are here. Do you understand, Abelone? I think you must understand.

Book Two

Now the tapestries of the Lady with the Unicorn are also no longer in the old castle of Boussac. The time has come when everything is coming out of the houses, they can no longer retain anything. Danger has become more safe than safety. No one from the race of the Delle Vistes walks beside one and has the race in his blood. They are all gone. No one speaks your name, Pierre d'Aubisson, great grandmaster from an ancient house, who perhaps willed these images to be woven that praise everything and expose nothing. (Alas, that poets have ever written differently of women, more literally, as they thought. It is certain that this is all we were allowed to know.) Now one accidentally emerges among accidental things and almost takes fright at not being invited. But other people are there and walk past, even if they are never many. The young people hardly pause, unless it happens somehow to belong to their specialty to have seen these things once, looking for this or that particular quality.

But at times one finds young girls in front of them. For there is a host of young girls in museums who have left the houses somewhere that retain nothing any more. They find themselves in front of these tapestries and forget themselves a little. They have always felt that this existed, such a gentle life of slower, never completely explained gestures, and they dimly remember that they even thought for a while that this life would be theirs. But then they quickly take out a sketchbook and begin to draw, it doesn't matter what, one of the flowers or a small, cheerful animal. It did not matter, they had been instructed; whatever it happened to be. And it really does not matter: only that drawing takes place, that is the main thing; for the reason they left home one day, rather abruptly, was to draw. They are of good family. But if now they raise their arms while they are drawing it appears that their dress is not buttoned up in back, or not completely. There are a few buttons one cannot reach. For when this dress was made there was not yet any talk of their suddenly leaving by themselves. Within the family there is always someone for such buttons. But here, my God, who should waste time on such a thing in such a big city. One would have to have a girl friend, but such friends are in the same situation, and it would still amount to having to button up each other's dresses. That is absurd, and reminds one of the family one does not want to be reminded of.

There is no avoiding that sometimes, while one is drawing, one considers whether it would not have been possible to stay. If one could have been pious, heartily pious in the same tempo as the others. But it seemed so silly to attempt that together. The path has somehow become narrower: families can no longer attain God. So there remained only various other things that, if need be, one could share. But then, if one shared honestly, the individual mattered so little that it was a disgrace. And if one cheated in sharing, quarrels arose. No, it is really better to draw, it doesn't matter what. Given time, the likeness will emerge. And art, if one gradually learns to do it this way, is something really enviable.

But in the strain of the task they have undertaken, these young girls, they no longer get around to looking up. They do not notice how with all their drawing they are doing nothing but suppressing in themselves the unalterable life that radiantly, in its infinite unutterability, opens up before them in these woven images. They do not want to believe it. Now, when so much else is changing, they want to change themselves. They are on the point of giving up on themselves and thinking about themselves the way that men might perhaps talk about them when they are not there. That seems to these girls their path to progress. They are already almost convinced that one seeks a gratification, and then another, and a gratification that is still stronger; that that is what life consists of, if one does not want to lose it in some absurd way. They have already begun to look around, to seek; they, whose strength has always consisted in being found.

That comes about, I believe, because they are tired. For centuries women have accomplished the totality of love, they have always played the whole dialog, both roles. For the man has only repeated after them, and badly. And made their learning difficult with his distractedness, his negligence, his jealousy that was also a kind of negligence. But women nevertheless persevered day and night, and grew in love and misery. And from among them, under the pressure of endless needs, there arose the powerful lovers who, while they summoned him, survived the man; who grew beyond him when he did not return, like Gaspara Stampa or the Portuguese nun, who did not let up until their torment veered around to an astringent, icy gloriousness that could be held back no longer. We know about this person and that because there are letters that through some miracle survive, or books with accusing or plaintive poems, or portraits in a gallery that look at us through tears, portraits in which the painters succeeded because they did not know what it was. But there are countless more of them: those who burned their letters and others who no longer had the strength to write them. Old women who had become hard, with a precious kernel inside that they concealed. Shapeless women who had become stout, who, grown stout from exhaustion, let themselves become like their husbands and yet were quite different inside, there where their love had been working, in the darkness. Giving birth who never wanted to give birth, and when they finally died from the eighth birth they had the gestures and lightness of girls looking forward to love. And those who remained beside ragers and drinkers because they had found the means to be as far from them inwardly as never elsewhere; and when they came among people they could not restrain it and shone as if they always associated with saints. Who can say how many there were, and which. It is as if they had destroyed in advance the words by which one could grasp them.

But now, when so much is changing, is it not up to us to change ourselves? Could we not try to develop ourselves a little, and slowly, gradually, take upon ourselves our share of the work in love? We have been spared all its hardship, and so it has slipped among our distractions, as a piece of genuine lace falls into a child's box of toys, and delights and no longer delights and finally lies there among the broken and disassembled things in worse state than everything else. Like all dilettantes we have been spoiled by easy enjoyment, and are reputed to be masters. But what if we despised our successes, what if we were to begin from the very beginning to learn the work of love that has always been done for us? What if we went off and became beginners, now that so much is changing.

Now I also know how it was when Mama unrolled the small pieces of lace. She had taken for her own use just one of the drawers in Ingeborg's desk.

"Do you want to see them, Malte?" she said and was happy, as if she were about to receive as a present everything that was in the small, yellow-lacquered drawer. And then from sheer anticipation she could not unwrap the silk paper. I had to do it every time. But I too became quite excited when the lace appeared. The pieces were wound around a wooden rod, which was quite invisible under all the lace. And now we slowly unwound them and looked at the patterns and how they played out, and were startled a little when one came to an end. They stopped so suddenly.

First there were selvages of Italian work, knotty pieces with drawn-out threads in which everything constantly repeated, distinct as in a peasant's garden. Then suddenly a whole series of our glances was fenced in by Venetian needlepoint, as if we were convents, or prisons. But we were freed again and peered far into gardens that became ever more artificial, until one's eyes became heavy and moist, as in a greenhouse: magnificent plants we did not know put out gigantic leaves, vines were reaching for one another as though they were dizzy, and the big open flowers of the Points d'Alençon misted everything with their pollen. Suddenly, quite tired and confused, one stepped out into the long path of the Valenciennes, and it was winter and early in the day, and there was hoarfrost. And one pushed through the snowy bushes of the Binche and came to places where no one had walked; the twigs hung down so peculiarly that there might well have been a grave beneath them, but we concealed that from each other. The cold pressed in on us more and more, and finally, when we got to the small, extremely delicate Klöppel laces, Mama said: "Oh, now we'll get frost-flowers on our eyes," and so we did, for inwardly it was very warm in us.

We both sighed over the rolling up, it was a lengthy task, but we did not want to leave it to anyone else.

"Just think if we had to make them," Mama said and looked positively frightened. That was something I could not imagine. I caught myself thinking of small animals constantly spinning, whom one left in peace for that purpose. No, of course it had been women.

"Those who made it surely got to heaven," I said admiringly. I remember it occurred to me that it had been a long time since I asked about heaven. Mama breathed in relief, the laces were again rolled up together.

After a while, when I had already forgotten it, she said quite slowly: "Got to heaven? I believe they are definitely there. If one looks at it that way, it might well be an eternal blessedness. One knows so little about it."

Often, when they had visitors, it was said that the Schulins were cutting back. The big old castle had burned down several years before, and now they lived in the two narrow side-wings and were cutting back. But hospitality was in their blood. They could not give it up. If someone came to us unexpectedly he probably came from the Schulins; and if someone suddenly looked at his watch and, startled, had to rush off, he was surely expected at Lystager.

Mama already never went anywhere any more, but that was something the Schulins could not comprehend; there was nothing for it but to drive over there. It was in December, after a few early snowfalls; the sleigh had been ordered for three o'clock, I was to go along. But at our house we never left on time. Mama, who didn't like having the coach announced, usually came down much too early, and when she found no one always thought of something she should have attended to long before, and began to search for or arrange things somewhere upstairs, so that it was hardly possible to get hold of her again. At last everyone was standing around waiting. And when she was finally settled in the coach and packed in, it turned out that something had been forgotten, and Sieversen had to be fetched; for only Sieversen knew where it was. But then we suddenly set off before Sieversen came back.

On that day it had never really got brighter. The trees stood as if they didn't know what to do in the fog, and there was something opinionated about driving among them. Now and then it silently began to snow again, and it seemed as if the last bit had been erased and as if one were driving into a white page. There was nothing but the ringing of the bells, and one could not really say where it came from. There was a moment when it stopped, as if the last sleighbell had been expended; but then it gathered again and became coherent and strewed itself again from out of its fullness. One might have imagined the church steeple on the left. But suddenly there was the outline of the grounds, high, almost above one, and one found oneself in the long drive. The sound no longer fell away entirely; it was as if it were hanging in clusters on the trees left and right. Then one swung around and drove around something and past something on the right and stopped in the middle.

Georg had completely forgotten that the big house was not there, and for all of us at that moment it was there. We walked up the stairs leading to the old terrace, and were only surprised that it was completely dark. Suddenly a door opened, down below on the left, and someone called out: "This way!" and raised and swung a misty lantern. My father laughed: "We're wandering around here like ghosts," and helped us back down the steps.

"But there was a house there just now," Mama said, and could not get used quite so quickly to Vera Shulin, who had run out warm and laughing. Then of course one had to hasten inside, and there was no time to think of the great house any longer. We took off our coats in a narrow vestibule, and then were in the midst of things across the hall, in the warmth and under the lamps.

These Schulins were a powerful race of independent women. I don't know if there were any sons. I only remember three sisters; the oldest, who had been married to a Marchese in Naples from whom she parted slowly and through many court trials. Then came Zoë, of whom it was said that there was nothing she did not know. And above all there was Vera, this warm Vera; God knows what has happened to her. The Countess, a Narischkin, was really the fourth sister, and in certain respects the youngest. She knew nothing and had to be continually instructed by her children. And the good Count Schulin felt as if he were married to all these women, and went around and kissed them as the occasion offered.

At first he laughed aloud, and greeted us at length. I was handed on to the ladies and poked and questioned. But I had firmly determined that when that was over I would somehow slip out and look for the great house. I was convinced that it was there that day. Getting away was not so difficult; one crawled under all the coats like a dog, and the door to the vestibule was still open a crack. But the outside door refused to yield. It had several devices, chains and bolts, that in my haste I did not manipulate properly. Suddenly they opened, but with a loud noise, and before I got outside I was grabbed and pulled back.

"Stop, no running away here!" Vera Schulin was amused. She bent down to me, but I was determined to betray nothing to this warm person. But she, when I said nothing, promptly assumed that a call of nature had driven me to the door: she seized my hand and started off, trying half familiarly, half arrogantly to pull me somewhere. This intimate misunderstanding offended me exceedingly. I tore myself loose and looked at her angrily. "I want to see the house." She did not understand.

"The great house outside by the steps."

"Silly," she said, reaching out for me. "There is no house there any more." I insisted that there was.

"We'll go there in the daylight," she proposed, compromising. "One can't go crawling around there now. There are holes, and right in back are Papa's fish ponds that aren't allowed to freeze. You'll fall in and turn into a fish."

With this she pushed me before her back into the bright rooms. Everyone was sitting and talking, and I looked at them all in turn: of course they would only go if it's not there, I thought contemptuously; if Mama and I lived here, it would always be there. Mama looked distracted while everyone was talking at once. She was surely thinking of the house.

Zoë sat down beside me and asked me questions. She had smooth features in which comprehension renewed itself from time to time, as if she were constantly understanding something. My father was sitting somewhat inclined to the right and listening to the Marchioness, who was laughing. Count Schulin stood between Mama and his wife and was relating something. But I saw the Countess interrupt him in the middle of a sentence.

"No, child, you're just imagining it," the Count said good-naturedly, but suddenly he had the same anxious face, which he extended over both ladies. The Countess was not to be dissuaded from her so-called imagining. She was concentrating like someone who does not want to be disturbed. She made small, dismissive motions with her soft beringed hands, someone said "ssh," and suddenly it became very still.

The large objects from the old house pressed in behind the people, much too close. The heavy family silver shone and bulged as if one were seeing it through a magnifying glass. My father looked around discomfited.

"Mama smells something," Vera Schulin said behind him, "we must all be quiet, she smells with her ears." But she herself stood there with raised eyebrows, alert and all nose.

In this connection, the Schulins had been a little peculiar since the fire. A smell arose every moment in the narrow, overheated rooms, and then its source had to be investigated and everyone gave his opinion. Zoë busied herself with the stove, matter-of-factly and conscientiously; the Count went around and stood for a bit in every corner, and pausing, said each time: "It's not here." The Countess had stood up but didn't know where to search. My father slowly turned around in a circle, as if he had the smell behind him. The Marchioness, who had immediately assumed that it was a nasty odor, held her handkerchief before her face and looked from one to the other to see whether it had gone away. "Here, here," Vera called out from time to time, as if she had found it. And around every word it became remarkably quiet. For my part, I had diligently smelled along. But suddenly (was it the heat in the rooms or so much light so close) I was overcome for the first time in my life by something like the fear of ghosts. It struck me that all the distinctly grown-up people who had just been talking and laughing were going around bent over and busying themselves with something invisible; that they were admitting that something was there that they did not see. And it was horrible that it was stronger than all of them.

My fear increased. It seemed to me that what they were looking for could suddenly break out of me like a rash; and then they would see it and point at me. In desperation I looked over at Mama. She was sitting strangely upright, it seemed she was waiting for me. Hardly had I reached her and felt that she was trembling inwardly, than I knew that the house was just now perishing again.

"Malte, coward," it laughed somewhere. It was Vera's voice. But we did not let go of each other and bore it together; and we remained that way, Mama and I, until the house was entirely gone again.

But among all the almost incomprehensible experiences, the best were the birthdays. One already knew that it pleased life not to make distinctions; but on this day one arose with a right to joy that was not to be doubted. Apparently this right had formed in one quite early, at the time one reaches out for everything and gets absolutely everything, and when with an unshakable power of imagination one intensifies the object one happens to be grasping with the intensity of the primary color of the desire that happens to be uppermost at the moment.

But then suddenly come those peculiar birthdays when, completely attached to the consciousness of this right, one sees other people becoming uncertain. One would like to be dressed the way one used to be and then accept whatever came. But hardly is one awake than someone calls outside that the cake isn't there yet; or one hears something break while the table with the presents is being set up in the next room; or someone comes in and leaves the door open and one sees everything before one should. That is the moment when something like an operation happens to one. A short, insanely painful incision. But the hand that does it is practiced and firm. It is quickly over. And hardly has it been got through when one no longer thinks of oneself; it's a question of saving the birthday, of observing others, anticipating their mistakes, strengthening them in the illusion that they are doing everything splendidly. They don't make it easy for one. It turns out that they are of an unparalleled awkwardness, almost empty-headed. They manage to come in with some packages or other meant for someone else; one runs toward them and then has to act as if one were running around the room for exercise, with no particular purpose. They want to surprise one, and putting on a superficial imitation of expectation lift up the bottom layer of the toybox, which contains nothing but wood shavings, and then one must ease their embarrassment. Or if it was something mechanical, they overwind what they have given you the first time they try to start it. So it is good if, before it's too late, one unobtrusively practices pushing an overwound mouse or the like forward with one's foot; in this way one can often fool them and help them over their shame.

One managed all that, finally, as one was expected to, even without any special talent. Talent was really only necessary if someone had taken special pains and, self-important and benevolent, had brought a joy, and one saw already from a distance that it was a joy for someone quite different, a completely alien joy, one could not even think who it might be suitable for: so alien was it.

That one told stories, really told them, that must have been before my time. I have never heard anyone tell stories. In the days when Abelone told me about Mama's youth, it turned out that she could not tell a story. Old Count Brahe is said to have still been able to. I'll write down what Abelone knew about it.

There must have been a time when Abelone was a very young girl in which she was animated in her own expansive way. At that time the Brahes were living in town, in the Bredgade, and entertained fairly often. When she went up to her room late in the evening, she thought she was tired like the others. But then she suddenly felt the window, and, if I understood aright, she could stand for hours facing the night and think: it is speaking to me. "I stood there like a prisoner," she said, "and the stars were freedom." Then she could go to sleep without difficulty. The expression "to fall asleep" was not right for this year of girlhood. Sleep was something that rose up with one, and from time to time one had one's eyes open and lay on a new surface that was by no means the uppermost one. And then one was up before day, even in winter, when the others came to the late breakfast belated and sleepy. Evenings, when it got dark, there were always candles for everyone, ordinary candles. But these two candles, quite early in the new darkness with which everything began again, these one had for oneself. They stood in their low double candlestick and shone quietly through the small, oval tulle shades painted with roses, which from time to time had to be adjusted. That was not at all bothersome; for one thing, one was in no hurry at all, and then it happened that sometimes one had to look up and think, when one was composing a letter or writing in one's diary, which at some earlier time had been begun in a quite different hand, anxious and lovely.

Count Brahe lived quite apart from his daughters. He considered it a fantasy if someone insisted on sharing life with others. ("Well, sharing—" he said.) But he did not take it amiss when people talked to him about his daughters; he listened attentively, as if they lived in some other city.

So it was quite extraordinary that one day, after breakfast, he motioned Abelone over to him: "We have the same habits, it appears, I too am up writing quite early. You can help me." Abelone still remembered it as if it had been yesterday.

Already the next morning she was conducted to her father's study, which had the reputation of being inaccessible. She did not have time to look around, for she was made to sit down immediately opposite the Count at the desk, which seemed to her like a plain, with books and writing utensils as villages.

The Count dictated. Those who maintained that Count Brahe was writing his memoirs were not entirely wrong. But these memoirs did not deal with political or military memories, as people were suspensefully expecting. "Those I forget," the old gentleman said curtly, if someone spoke to him about such facts. But what he did not want to forget was his childhood. That was his goal. And it seemed quite in order, in his opinion, that that quite distant time now gained the upper hand in him, that time which, when he turned his glance inward, lay there as in a bright northern summer night, intensified and sleepless.

Sometimes he jumped up and spoke into the candles so that they flickered. Or whole sentences had to be crossed out, and then he agitatedly paced up and down, his nile-green silk dressing gown billowing. During all this there was another person present, Sten, the Count's old Jutland servant, whose task it was, when grandfather jumped up, to quickly lay his hands over the loose pages that, covered with notes, lay about on the desk. His Grace had the notion that paper today was worthless, that it was far too light and would fly about on the slightest provocation. And Sten, of whom one only saw the tall upper half, shared this suspicion and sat, so to speak, on his hands, blind to the light and serious as a night bird.

This Sten spent his Sunday afternoons reading Swedenborg, and none of the other servants had ever wanted to enter his room, because it was said that he was reciting. Sten's family had consorted with spirits from far back, and Sten had been quite particularly destined for this communication. Something appeared to his mother on the night she bore him. He had large, round eyes, and the other end of his glance penetrated behind the person it was resting on. Abelone's father often asked him about ghosts, the way one usually asks about someone's family: "Are they coming, Sten?" he said benevolently. "It is good if they come."

For a few days the dictation took its course. But then Abelone could not write "Eckernförde." It was a proper name, and she had never heard it. The Count, who had long been seeking a pretext to give up writing, which was too slow for his memories, pretended to be indignant.

"She can't write it," he said sharply, "and others won't be able to read it. And will they, in any event, *see* what I am saying here?" he continued angrily, without taking his eyes off Abelone.

"Will they see this Saint-Germain? he shouted at her. "Did we say Saint-Germain? Cross it out. Write: The Marquis of Belmare."

Abelone crossed out and wrote. But the Count continued speaking so rapidly that one couldn't keep up.

"He couldn't stand children, this excellent Belmare, but me he took on his knee, small as I was, and I got it into my head to bite his diamond buttons. That amused him. He laughed and raised my head so that we were looking each other in the eye: 'You have splendid teeth,' he said, 'enterprising teeth . . .' But I took note of his eyes. Later I have been here and there. I have seen all sorts of eyes, of that you can be sure: never again such eyes. Those eyes needed nothing external, it resided within them. Have you heard of Venice? Good. I'm telling you, those eyes would have seen Venice into this room so it would have been here like this desk. I was once sitting in the corner listening to him tell my father about Persia, I sometimes think my hands still have the smell of it. My father esteemed him, and His Highness, the Landgrave, was something like his pupil. But of course there were enough people who held it against him that he only believed in the past if it was *in* him. They couldn't understand that that stuff only means something if one is born with it.

"Books are empty!" the Count shouted, gesturing angrily at the walls. "Blood, that's what matters, that's what one has to be able to read in them. He had strange tales with peculiar pictures in them, this Belmare; he could open wherever he wanted, there was always something described there; no page in his blood was passed over. And when he withdrew from time to time and paged through them alone, he came to the places about the making of gold and about precious stones and about colors. Why should that not have been in them? Surely it must be there someplace.

"He could have lived with his truth quite well, this fellow, if he had been alone. But it was no trifle to be alone with such a truth. And he was not so tasteless as to invite people so that they would visit him for his truth; it was not to be talked about: for that he was much too oriental. 'Adieu, Madame,' he said to her truthfully, 'until another time. Perhaps in a thousand years you will be stronger and less disturbed. Your beauty is just at an early stage, Madame,' he said, and it was no mere politeness. With that he went off and designed his menagerie for people, a sort of zoo for the larger kind of lies that had never been seen among us, and a palm court of exaggerations and a small, manicured fig grove of false secrets. People came from all sides, and he walked around with diamond clasps on his shoes and devoted himself entirely to his guests.

"A superficial existence: how so? Basically it was chivalry toward his lady, and it enabled him to conserve himself pretty well."

For some time the old man had not been talking to Abelone, whom he had forgotten. He paced back and forth furiously, casting challenging glances at Sten, as if at a certain moment Sten would transform himself into the man he was thinking of. But Sten was not yet transforming himself.

"One had to *see* him," Count Brahe went on, obsessed. "There was a time when he was quite visible, although in many cities the letters he received were not addressed to anyone: only the place was named, nothing else. But I have seen him.

"He was not handsome," the Count laughed peculiarly, quickly. "Nor what people call significant, or aristocratic: there were always people beside him who were more aristocratic. He was rich: but for him that was only a notion, not something that defined him. He was well-formed, although others kept themselves better. Of course, at that time I could not judge whether he was clever, or this or that which is thought to be important—: but he *was*."

The Count, trembling, stopped and made a motion as if placing something in space that stayed there. At that moment he perceived Abelone.

"Do you see him?" he barked at her. And suddenly he seized one of the silver candelabras and shone it blindingly into her face.

Abelone remembered that she had seen him.

In the following days Abelone was regularly summoned, and after this incident the dictating went on much more calmly. The Count gathered from all sorts of papers his earliest memories of the Bernstorff circle, in which his father had played a certain role. Abelone was now so accustomed to the peculiarities of her task that whoever saw the two of them could easily mistake their purposeful togetherness for a genuine intimacy.

Once, as Abelone was about to leave, the old gentleman went up to her as if he were holding his hands behind his back with a surprise: "Tomorrow we will write about Julie Reventlow," he said, relishing the words. "She was a saint."

Apparently Abelone looked at him incredulously.

"Yes, yes, all that is still to come," he insisted in a commanding tone, "all that, Countess Abel."

He took Abelone's hands and opened them like a book.

"She had the stigmata," he said. "Here and here." And with his cold finger he tapped hard and quickly in both her palms.

Abelone did not know the term "stigmata." It will become clear, she thought; she was quite impatient to hear about the saint her father had still been able to see. But she was sent for no more, not the next morning and not later, either.—

"In your house they often talked about Countess Reventlow," Abelone concluded abruptly when I begged her to tell more. She looked tired; she also maintained she had forgotten most of it. "But I still feel the places sometimes." She smiled and couldn't stop, looking almost curiously into her empty hands.

Even before my father's death everything had changed. Ulsgaard was no longer in our possession. My father died in town, in an apartment that seemed to me hostile and strange. At that time I was already abroad, and came too late.

He was laid out between two rows of tall candles in a room overlooking the courtyard. The smell of flowers was incomprehensible, like many voices talking at once. His handsome face, in which the eyes had been closed, bore an expression of polite recall. He was clothed in the uniform of Master of the Hunt, but for some reason the white ribbon instead of the blue had been placed on him. His hands were not folded, they lay diagonally across each other, looking counterfeit and meaningless. I had been hastily told that he had suffered a great deal: nothing of that was to be seen. His features were cleaned like the furniture in a hotel room from which someone had checked out. I felt as if I had already seen him dead rather often: so well did I know all that.

The only thing that was new was the environment, in an unpleasant way. New was this oppressive room, facing windows opposite, apparently the windows of other people. It was new that Sieversen came in from time to time but did nothing. Sieversen had grown old. Then I was to have breakfast. Several times I was told it was ready. I had no interest in breakfasting that day. I didn't notice that they wanted me out of the way; finally, when I didn't leave, Sieversen somehow brought out that the doctors were there. I did not understand why. They still had something to do, Sieversen said, looking at me closely with reddened eyes. Then two men came in, somewhat hurriedly: they were the doctors. The one in front lowered his head with a jerk, as if he had horns and was about to charge, to look at us over his glasses: first at Sieversen, then at me.

He bowed with a student's formality. "The Master of the Hunt had one more wish," he said, in precisely the same way as he had come in; one again had the feeling that he was hurried. I somehow forced him to direct his gaze through his glasses. His colleague was a plump, thin-skinned blond person; it occurred to me it would be easy to make him blush. A pause ensued. It was odd that the Master of the Hunt still had wishes.

Involuntarily I glanced again at the handsome, regular face. And then I knew that he wanted certainty. Basically that is what he had always wanted. Now he was to get it.

"You are here to penetrate the heart: please."

I bowed and stepped back. The two doctors bowed simultaneously and immediately began to decide how to proceed. Someone was already moving the candles aside. But the older doctor again took a few steps toward me. From a certain close distance he leaned forward, to save himself the last bit of the way, and looked at me angrily.

"It is not necessary," he said, "that is, I mean, it would perhaps be better if you . . ."

He seemed disheveled and worn out in his thrifty and hasty posture. I bowed once more; it happened that I bowed a second time.

"Thank you," I said curtly. "I won't disturb."

I knew that I would bear this, and that there was no reason for me to withdraw from this affair. It had to come to this. Perhaps that was what it all meant. Also, I had never seen what it was like for someone to be penetrated through the breast. It seemed to me proper not to refuse such a remarkable experience where it was taking place casually and unconditionally. Already at that time I no longer really believed in disappointments, so there was nothing to be feared.

No, no, one can imagine nothing in the world, not the least thing. Everything is composed of so many isolated details that are not to be foreseen. In one's imagining one passes over them and hasty as one is doesn't notice that they are missing. But realities are slow and indescribably detailed.

Who, for instance, would have thought of this resistance. Hardly had the broad, high breast been exposed than the small hasty man had fixed on the spot in question. But the instrument, quickly placed there, did not penetrate. I had the feeling that suddenly all time had fled from the room. We were like in a painting. But then time rushed on with a small, gliding noise, and there was more time than was consumed. Suddenly there was a knocking somewhere. I had never heard such knocking: a warm, muffled, doubled knocking. My hearing passed it on, and at the same time I saw that the doctor had struck bottom. But it took a while for the two impressions to come together in me. So, so, I thought, now it has penetrated. The knocking was, in its tempo, almost gloating.

I looked at the doctor whom I had now known for such a long time. No, he was completely composed: a man who worked quickly and matter-of-factly, who had to go somewhere else right away. He showed no trace of enjoyment or satisfaction. Only on his left temple a few hairs had stood up, from some sort of old instinct. He cautiously pulled the instrument out, and there was something like a mouth out of which blood emerged, twice in succession, as if it were saying something in two syllables. With an elegant motion the young blond doctor quickly dabbed it up with his cotton. And now the wound remained quiet, like a closed eye.

It is to be assumed that I bowed once again, this time without really being aware of it. At least I was astonished to find myself alone. Someone had rearranged the uniform, and the white ribbon lay over it as before. But now the Master of the Hunt was dead, and not only he. Now the heart had been bored through, our heart, the heart of our race. Now it was over. So that was the breaking of the helmet: "Brigge today and nevermore," something in me said.

I was not thinking of my heart. And when it occurred to me later I knew with certainty, for the first time, that it was not involved in this. Mine was an individual heart. It was already at work beginning from the beginning.

I know that I imagined I could not leave right away. First everything has to be taken care of, I said to myself. *What* had to be taken care of was not clear to me. There was as good as nothing that needed to be done. I walked around in the city and saw that it had changed. I found it pleasant to walk out of the hotel in which I was staying and to see that it was now a city for grownups, who drew themselves up, almost as if for a stranger. It had all become a little small, and I walked out the Langelinie as far as the lighthouse and back again. When I came to the neighborhood around the Amaliengade, it could happen that something emanated from some place one had recognized for years and that was trying to exert its power once more. There were certain corner windows or archways or lanterns that knew a lot about one and threatened one with it. I looked them in the face and let them know that I was staying at the Hotel Phoenix and could leave again at any moment. But this did not quiet my conscience. The suspicion arose in me that not one of these influences or contexts had really been overcome. One day one had secretly abandoned them, unfinished as they were. Childhood too, in a certain sense, would still have to be accomplished, if one did not want to consider it abandoned forever. And while I understood how I had lost it, I felt at the same time that I would never have anything else I could call upon.

I spent a few hours every day in Dronningens Tvaergade, in narrow rooms that looked offended, like all rented rooms in which someone has died. I paced back and forth between the desk and the big white-tiled stove, burning the Master of the Hunt's papers. I had begun to throw into the fire all his letters the way they were bundled together, but the small packets were too firmly tied and only charred at the edges. It took an effort to loosen them. Most had a strong, convincing scent that penetrated me as if it were trying to awaken memories in me as well. I had none. Then it might happen that photographs slipped out that were heavier than the rest. These photographs burned with incredible slowness. I don't know how it happened, suddenly I imagined that Ingeborg's picture could be among them. But as often as I looked, they were mature, magnificent, strikingly beautiful women, who turned my thoughts in another direction. For it appeared that I was not entirely without memories. It was just such eyes in which I sometimes found myself, when, at the time I was growing up, I crossed the street with my father. Then, from the interior of a coach, they could envelop me with a glance from which it was difficult to emerge. Now I knew that at that time they were comparing me to him, and that the comparison did not favor me. Certainly not, the Master of the Hunt had nothing to fear from comparisons.

It may be that I now know something that he feared. I will tell how I arrived at this assumption. There was a paper at the bottom of his wallet, folded long ago, crumbly, coming apart at the folds. I read it before I burned it. It was in his best hand, written confidently and evenly, but I saw right away that it was only a copy.

"Three hours before his death," it began, and dealt with the death of Christian the Fourth. Of course I can't repeat what it said word for word. The doctor and Chamberlain Wormius helped him to his feet. He stood somewhat uncertainly, but he was standing, and they dressed him in his quilted nightdress. Then he suddenly sat down at the end of the bed and said something. It was incomprehensible. The doctor held on to his left hand so that the king would not sink back on the bed. Thus they sat, and the king said from time to time, dully and with effort, the incomprehensible. At last the doctor began to speak to him; he hoped gradually to find out what the king meant. After a while the king interrupted him, and suddenly said quite clearly: "O doctor, doctor, what is his name?" The doctor ransacked his brains.

"Sperling, most Gracious Majesty."

But that wasn't what he meant. As soon as the king heard that he was understood, he tore open his right eye, the remaining one, and with his entire countenance said the single word his tongue had been forming for hours, the only word that still had meaning: "døden," he said, "døden."[17]

There was nothing else on the paper. I read it several times before I burned it. And it occurred to me that my father had suffered much at the end. That was what I had been told.

Since then I have thought a good deal about the fear of death, not without taking into account certain experiences of my own. I believe I can say I have felt it. It came over me in the busy city, in the midst of people, often for no reason. But often too the causes piled up: when for example someone died on a bench and everyone stood around looking at him, and he was already beyond fear: then I had his fear. Or that time in Naples: there was this young person who sat opposite me in the trolley car and died. At first it looked as if she had fainted, we even went on for a while. But then there was no doubt that we had to stop. And the vehicles behind us stopped and were backed up as if

17   Danish: Death

there would never be any further motion in this direction again. The pale, fat girl could have died quietly, leaning on her neighbor. But her mother would not allow it. She made all sorts of difficulties. She disarranged the girl's clothes and poured something into the mouth that no longer retained anything. She rubbed on her forehead a liquid someone had handed her, and when the girl's eyes rolled a little she began shaking her so her glance would face forward again. She screamed into these eyes that did not hear, she pushed and pulled the whole thing back and forth like a doll, and finally she pulled back and struck the fat face with all her strength so that it would not die. At that time I was afraid.

But I had been afraid even earlier, too. For example, when my dog died. The same dog that blamed me once and for all. He was very ill. I had been kneeling beside him the whole day when suddenly he barked sharply, once and toward the back, as he was accustomed to do whenever a stranger entered the room. For that case such a bark had been, so to speak, agreed upon between us, and I involuntarily glanced toward the door. But it was already in him. Concerned, I sought his glance, and he too sought mine, but not to take leave. He looked at me bitterly and estranged. He was reproaching me for having let it in. He was convinced I could have prevented it. Now it came out that he had always overestimated me. And there was no longer time to enlighten him. He looked at me estranged and alone until it was over.

Or I was afraid when in autumn, after the first nights of frost, the flies would come into the room and recover one more time in the warmth. They were oddly dried out, and recoiled from their own humming; one could see that they no longer really knew what they were doing. They sat there for hours and let themselves go, until it occurred to them that they were still alive; then they blindly flung themselves someplace but did not understand what they should do there, and one kept hearing them fall down here, there, and everywhere. Finally they were crawling all over and slowly making the whole room die.

But I could be afraid even when I was alone. Why should I act as if there had not been those nights when I sat up from the fear of death and clung to the idea of sitting up because it was at least something alive: the dead don't sit up. That always happened in one of those chance rooms that immediately left me in the lurch when things were going badly for me, as if they feared being interrogated and involved in my nasty affairs. There I sat, and apparently I looked so terrible that nothing had the courage to acknowledge me. Not even the light, which I had just done the favor of turning on, wanted anything to do with me. It simply burned for itself, as in an empty room. My last hope then was always the window. I imagined that there could still be something outside that belonged to me, even now, even in this sudden poverty of dying. But hardly had I looked out when I wished that the window had been barricaded shut, like the wall. For now I knew that outside things were going on indifferently, always the same, that outside too there was nothing but my loneliness. The loneliness that I had brought on myself and to whose size my heart no longer bore any relation. People from whom I had once gone away came to mind, and I did not understand how one could abandon people.

My God, my God, if such nights lie ahead of me, leave me at least one of the thoughts that I could sometimes think. What I am asking for is not so unreasonable, for I know that these thoughts have arisen directly from the fear because my fear was so great. When I was a boy they struck me in the face and told me that I was a coward. That was because I was still bad at fearing. But since then I have learned to fear with real fear, which only increases when the energy that produces it increases. We have no conception of this energy except in our fear. For it is so totally incomprehensible, so completely against us, that our brain dissolves at the spot where we strain to think it. And yet I have for some time believed that it is *our* energy, all our energy, which is still too strong for us. It is true we don't know this power, but isn't it precisely what is most our own about which we know the least? Sometimes I think to myself how heaven arose, and death: through our having pushed away from ourselves what is most precious in us, because there was so much else that needed doing beforehand and because it was not safe among us busy people. Now ages have passed this way and we have accustomed ourselves to lesser things. We no longer recognize our property and are horrified at how extreme it has grown in size. Can that not be?

I now understand very well moreover how one can carry around in one's wallet for years the description of a dying hour. It would not even have had to be an exceptional one; they all have something special about them. Can one for example not imagine someone copying out for himself how Felix Arvers died. It was in the hospital. He was dying gently and calmly, and the nun perhaps thought he was further along in it than he actually was. She called out some instruction quite loudly, where this or that was to be found. She was a rather uneducated nun; she had never seen the word "corridor," which at that moment was not to be avoided; so it happened that she said "collidor," thinking that that was what it was called. Thereupon Felix Arvers postponed his dying. It seemed to him that this had to be cleared up first. He became quite clearheaded and explained to her that it was "corridor." Then he died. He was a poet and hated the approximate; or perhaps he only cared about the truth; or it bothered him to take with him as his last impression that the world would continue on so negligently. That can no longer be ascertained. But one should not believe that it was pedantry. Otherwise the same reproach would apply to the saintly Jean de Dieu, who jumped up in his dying just in time to cut down in the garden the man who had just been hanged, news of which had in miraculous fashion penetrated the closed tension of his agony. He too was only concerned with the truth.

There is a being that is completely harmless if it passes before your eyes, you hardly notice it and immediately forget it again. But as soon as it gets into your hearing in some invisible fashion it develops there, it creeps out, as it were, and one has seen cases where it penetrated the brain and thrived devastatingly in that organ, like the canine pneumococcus that enters through the nose.

This being is the neighbor.

Now since I have been traveling about so much alone I have had countless neighbors; above and below, right and left, sometimes all four kinds at once. I could simply write the story of my neighbors; that would be a life's work. And then it would be more the story of the symptoms than of the disease that they have produced in me; but they share with all such beings of the sort that they are known only by the disturbances they cause in certain tissues.

I have had unpredictable neighbors and very regular ones. I have sat and tried to find out the principle of the former; for it was clear that they too had one. And if the punctual ones happened to stay out in the evening I pictured to myself what might have happened to them, and left my light burning and worried like a young wife. I have had neighbors who hated intensely and neighbors involved in passionate love; or I experienced how the one suddenly turned into the other in the middle of the night, and then of course there was no thought of sleep. One could also observe that sleep is by no means so frequent as one thinks. My two neighbors in St. Petersburg, for example, were not much interested in sleep. One stood and played the violin, and I am certain that while he did so he was looking over into the intensely awake houses that never ceased being bright in the improbable August nights. About the other neighbor, on the right, I knew at least that he was lying down; in my time he no longer got up at all. He even kept his eyes closed, but one could not say that he was sleeping. He lay there and recited long poems, poems of Pushkin and Nekrassov, in the intonation with which children recite poems when it is demanded of them. And in spite of the music of my neighbor to the left, it was this neighbor with his poems that spun a cocoon in my head, and God knows what would have crawled out if the student who sometimes visited him had not one day knocked on the wrong door. He told me the story of his acquaintance, and it turned out to be reassuring in a way, in any event it was a literal, straightforward story that caused the many caterpillars of my suppositions to perish.

This minor official next door had, one Sunday, hit upon the idea that would solve a peculiar problem. He assumed that he would live for quite a long time, let's say another fifty years. The magnanimity he showed himself by this put him in a splendid mood. But now he wanted to outdo himself. He considered that one could transform these years into days, hours, and minutes, indeed, if one could bear it, into seconds, and he calculated and calculated, and came up with a sum like none he had ever seen. He was dizzy. He had to recover a little. Time was money, he had always heard it said, and he was surprised that a man who possessed so much time did not forthwith have someone to guard him. How easily he could be robbed. But then he got back his good, almost exuberant spirits, put on his fur coat in order to look larger and more imposing, and made himself a present of the entire fabulous capital, addressing himself a little patronizingly:

"Nikolai Kusmich," he said expansively, imagining himself sitting thin and scrawny without his fur coat on the horsehair sofa, "I hope, Nikolai Kusmich," he said, "you will not puff yourself up over your wealth. Always remember that's not the important thing. There are poor people who are thoroughly respectable; there are even impoverished aristocrats and generals' daughters who wander the streets selling things." And the benefactor adduced all sorts of well-known instances in the whole city.

The other Nikolai Kusmich, the one sitting on the horsehair sofa, the recipient of these gifts, did not appear at all high-spirited, one might assume that he would be reasonable about it. Indeed, he did not change anything in his modest, regular way of life, and now spent his Sundays ordering his accounts. But already after a few weeks it occurred to him that he was spending an incredible amount. I will cut back, he thought. He got up earlier, washed himself less thoroughly, drank his tea standing up, ran to the office and arrived much too early. Wherever he could he saved a little time. But by Sunday none of the savings had materialized. Then he realized that he had been cheated. I shouldn't have changed my money, he said to himself. How long one has in a year like this. But this disgraceful small change vanishes, one knows not how. And an ugly afternoon came when he sat in the corner of the sofa and waited for the man in the fur coat, from whom he wanted to demand his time back. He would bolt the door and not let him out until he had handed it over. "In notes on the bank," he wanted to say. "They can be for ten years, as far as I'm concerned." Four notes at ten per cent and one at five, and he could keep the rest, the devil take him. Yes, he was prepared to make him a present of the rest, just to forestall any difficulties. Irritated, he sat on the horsehair sofa and waited, but the man did not come. And he, Nikolai Kusmich, who a few weeks before had seen himself sitting there so casually, now that he was actually sitting there could not imagine the other Nikolai Kusmich, the one in the fur coat, the magnanimous one. Heaven knows what had happened to the fellow, apparently people had got wind of his swindles and he was now sitting in prison somewhere. Surely it was not only he himself to whom the man had brought misfortune. Such con men always work on a grand scale.

It occurred to him that there must be a government authority, a kind of time bank, where he could change at least a part of his paltry seconds. They were, after all, genuine. He had never heard of such an institution, but something of the sort could surely be found in the telephone book, under "T," or perhaps it was called "Bank for Time"; one could easily look under "B." Possibly the letter "I" should be considered, for it was to be assumed that it was an imperial institute, that would correspond to its importance.

Later Nikolai Kusmich always insisted that on that Sunday evening, although he was understandably in a quite depressed mood, he had not had anything to drink. He was completely sober when the following happened, to the extent one can say at all what did happen. Perhaps he had dozed off for a bit in his sofa corner, that is at least imaginable. This little nap brought him at first pure relief. I have gotten involved with numbers, he said to himself. Well, I understand nothing about numbers. But it is clear that one should not concede too much importance to them; they are, so to speak, only a mechanism of the state for the sake of order. No one has ever seen one anywhere but on paper. It was impossible, for instance, that one would meet a seven or a twenty-five at a party. They simply did not exist. And then this small confusion had arisen, from pure distraction: time and money, as if they could not be kept apart. Nikolai Kusmich almost laughed. It was good if one saw through it, and in time, that was the important thing, in time. Now it would be different. Time, that was an embarrassing affair. But was he the only one it concerned, wasn't the way he had discovered it also true for others, in seconds, even if they did not know it?

Nikolai Kusmich was not entirely free of malicious pleasure: time might in any case—he was about to think, but then something quite odd happened. Suddenly a breeze went by his face, it brushed past his ears, he felt it on his hands. He opened his eyes wide. The window was firmly shut. And as he sat there with eyes wide open in the dark room, he began to understand that what he was feeling was real time that was passing. He actually recognized them, all these seconds, equally tepid, one like the next, but quick, but quick. Heavens knows what they still intended to do. That this should have to happen to *him*, who felt every sort of wind as an insult. Now one would sit here and it would always go on this way, all one's life. He foresaw all the neuralgias he would catch, he was beside himself with rage. He jumped up, but the surprises were not yet over. Under his feet too something was in motion, not just one but several peculiar interacting motions. He froze in horror: could that be the earth? Indeed, it was the earth. Of course it was moving. That had been mentioned in school, it had been passed over rather hastily, and later it was gladly hushed up; it was not deemed proper to talk about. But now that he had become sensitive he was also feeling that too. Did other people feel it? Perhaps, but they didn't show it. Apparently it didn't bother them, these sea-folk. But precisely on this point Nikolai Kusmich was rather sensitive, he even avoided trolley cars. He staggered around the room as if on deck, and had to hold on right and left. Unfortunately he happened to think of the earth's tilted axis, too. No, he could not bear all these motions. He felt miserable. Lie down and keep still, he had once read somewhere. And since then Nikolai Kusmich had been lying down.

He lay and kept his eyes closed. And there were times, less agitated times, so to speak, when it was quite bearable. And then he thought up the business with the poems. One wouldn't believe how much that helped. If one recited such a poem slowly, uniformly emphasizing the endrimes, it gave one some kind of stability that one could actually see, inwardly, of course. It was a joy that he knew all these poems. But he had always been particularly interested in literature. The student, who had known him a long time, assured me that he did not complain about his condition. But over time he had developed an exaggerated admiration for those, like the student, who walked around and endured the motion of the earth.

I remember this story so exactly because it calmed me greatly. I can certainly say that I have never again had such an agreeable neighbor as this Nikolai Kusmich, who surely would also have admired me.

After this experience I decided that, in similar cases, I would immediately go for the facts. I noticed how simple and unburdening they were, as opposed to suppositions. As if I had not known that all our insights are after the fact, conclusions, nothing more. Right behind them a new page begins with something quite different, without carryover. What did the few facts help me now in the present case, facts that were effortlessly ascertained. I will have counted them up right away when I have said what is preoccupying me at the moment: that they have rather contributed to making my situation, which (as I now confess) was difficult, much more burdensome.

Let it be said to my credit that I have written much in these days: I have written in a desperate way. It's true that when I went out I did not look forward with pleasure to coming back home. I even made small detours, and in this way lost half an hour during which I could have been writing. I admit this was a weakness. But once I was in my room I had nothing to reproach myself with. I wrote, I had *my* life, and the life on the other side of the wall was a quite different life with which I had nothing in common: the life of a student of medicine studying for his exams. I was not facing anything like that, that was already a decisive difference. And otherwise too our circumstances were as different as possible. All that was clear to me. Up to the moment when I knew that it would come; then I forgot that we had nothing in common. I listened in such a way that my heart grew quite loud. I dropped everything and listened. And then it happened: I have never been wrong.

Almost everyone knows the noise that some kind of tinny, round thing, let's say the lid of a tin box, causes when it slips out of your hands. Usually it doesn't make much of a noise when it lands: it hits, rolls on its edge, and really only becomes unpleasant when the wobbling runs down and it tumbles noisily in all directions before coming to rest. So then: that's the whole story; some such tinny object fell next door, rolled, and lay still, after, at certain intervals, thumping.

Like all noises that are produced repetitively, this one too had organized itself inwardly; it transformed itself, it was never exactly the same. But precisely that spoke for its regularity. It could be violent or gentle or melancholy; it could happen head over heels, so to speak, or glide on endlessly before it came to rest. And the last wobble was always surprising. On the other hand, the final thud that followed had something almost mechanical about it. But it always marked off the noise differently, that seemed to be its task. Now I have a much better grasp of these details; the room beside mine is empty. He has gone home, to the provinces. He is to recuperate. I live on the top floor. To the right is another building, beneath me no one has moved in; I am without a neighbor.

In this frame of mind it almost surprises me that I didn't take the matter more casually. Although every time I had been warned in advance by my feeling. I could have used that to advantage. Don't be frightened, I would have had to say to myself, now it's coming; for I knew that I was never mistaken. But that lay perhaps precisely with the facts that I had been told; since I knew them, I was even more frightened. It touched me almost spectrally that what unleashed this noise was the small, slow, soundless motion with which his eyelid of its own accord lowered and closed over his right eye while he was reading. This was the important thing about his story, a trifle. He had already had to forego his examination several times, his ambition had become troubled, and the people at home were no doubt urging him on every time they wrote. So what else was there to do but pull oneself together. But then, a few months before a decision had to be made, this weakness had appeared; this small, impossible fatigue that was as ridiculous as if a window shade won't stay up. I am certain that for weeks he thought one ought to be able to control it. Otherwise I would never have hit upon the idea of offering him my will. For one day I understood that his was at an end. And after that, whenever I felt it coming on, I stood on my side of the wall and begged him to make use of it. And in time it became clear to me that he was responsive. Perhaps he ought not to have been, especially when one considers that it really didn't help. Even assuming that we held the thing at bay for a little, it still remains questionable whether he was actually able to make use of the moments we won this way. And as far as my expenditure of will was concerned, I began to feel it. I know I was asking myself whether it could go on this way just on the afternoon when someone came up to our floor. This always caused a lot of commotion in the narrow staircase of our small hotel. A little later it seemed to me that someone was going into my neighbor's room. Our doors were the last in the corridor, his diagonally right beside mine. I knew that he invited friends in from time to time, but, as I said, I had no interest at all in his affairs. It's possible his door was opened several more times, that people were coming and going. For that I was really not responsible.

But on this particular evening it was worse than ever. It was not yet very late, but I had already gone to bed exhausted; I thought it likely that I would sleep. Then I shot up as if someone had touched me. Immediately afterward it broke out.

There was jumping and rolling somewhere, and running and tottering and banging. The stamping was terrible. In between there was knocking from the floor below against the ceiling, clear and angry. Of course, the new tenant was disturbed too. Now: that must be his door. I was so awake that I thought I heard his door, although it was opened and closed with astonishing caution. It seemed to me as if the person were coming closer. He surely wanted to know what room it was coming from. What irritated me was his truly exaggerated consideration. He surely must have noticed that there was no thought of quiet in this house. Why for heaven's sake was he walking so softly? For a while I thought he was at my door; but then I perceived, and there was no doubt about it, that he was going in next door. He stepped in next door without further ado.

And now (how should I describe it?), now it became quiet. Quiet as when a pain ceases. A peculiar, sentient, tingling quiet, as if a wound were healing. I could have gone to sleep immediately; I could have got my breath and fallen asleep. Only my astonishment kept me awake. Someone was speaking next door, but that too was part of the stillness. One had to experience what this stillness was like, it can't be described. Outside too it was as if everything had been settled. I sat up, I listened, it was like being in the country. Dear God, I thought, his mother has come. She was sitting beside the lamp, she was talking to him, perhaps he had leaned his head slightly against her shoulder. Soon she would be putting him to bed. Now I understood the soft steps outside in the corridor. Oh, that that existed. A being like that, before whom doors yield quite differently than they do for us. Yes, now we could sleep.

I have almost entirely forgotten my neighbor. I see that it was not real sympathy that I had for him. Downstairs I sometimes ask in passing whether any news has come from him, and what news. And I am happy when it is good. But I exaggerate. I really have no need to know. That I sometimes feel a sudden impulse to walk in next door no longer has anything to do with him. It is only a step from my door to the other, and the room is not locked. It would interest me to see what it really looks like. One can easily imagine any sort of room, and often it more or less fits. But the room that one has next to one is always quite different than one thinks.

I tell myself that it is this circumstance that irritates me. But I know quite well that it is a certain tinny object that is waiting for me there. I have assumed that it really is a question of a box lid, although of course I might be mistaken. That does not unsettle me. It simply corresponds to my conception to blame the matter on a box lid. One can imagine that he did not take it with him. Apparently the room has been cleaned, the lid has been put back on its box, where it belongs. And now both together form the concept "box," round box to be precise, a simple, quite well-known notion. It seems to me as if I remember that it is standing on the mantelpiece, the two parts that constitute the box. Indeed they even stand in front of the mirror, so that behind them another box emerges, a deceptively similar, imaginary one. A box that is of no interest to us, but that an ape, for example, would grab for. Properly it would even be two apes, for the ape too would be doubled as soon as he got to the edge of the mantelpiece. Well, so it is the lid of this box that has it in for me.

Let's agree on this: the lid of a box, a healthy box, whose edge is curved no differently than its own, such a lid could have no other longing than to find itself on its box; this would have to be the utmost it could imagine; a satisfaction not to be surpassed, the fulfillment of all its desires. There is something positively ideal about its being placed patiently and softly and resting evenly on the small counter-bulge, feeling the intruding edge in itself, elastic and precisely as sharp as one's own edge is when one is lying there alone. But O how few lids there are that know how to appreciate this. Here one sees so clearly how confusing for things has been their consorting with people. People who, if one can fleetingly compare them with such lids, sit badly and for the most part sullenly on their activities.

Partly because in their haste they have not found the right boxes, partly because they have been placed on them angrily and askew, partly because the edges that belong together have been bent, each in a different manner. Let's say it quite straightforwardly: at bottom all they are thinking of is jumping down at the first possible moment, rolling, and being tinny. Where otherwise would all these so-called diversions come from, and the noise they cause?

Things have been looking on at this for centuries already. It's no wonder that they are spoiled, that they lose their taste for their natural, quiet purpose and want to exploit existence the way they see it exploited around them. They make attempts to withdraw from what they are used for, they become sullen and careless, and people are not at all surprised to catch them at some dissipation. That is something people know so well about themselves. People are angry because they are the stronger, because they think they have more right to change, because they feel themselves mimicked; but then they let the matter go as they let themselves go. But where there is a person who pulls himself together, a lonely person perhaps, who wants to rest roundly on himself day and night, he provokes contradiction, scorn, and hatred from the worn-out tools that in their bad conscience can no longer bear that something is pulling itself together and striving to realize itself. Then they gang together to upset, frighten, mislead him, and know that they can do it. Winking at each other they begin their seduction, which grows and grows into the inestimable, and instigate all beings and God himself against the one person who will perhaps survive: the saint.

How I understand now those strange paintings in which objects of limited but common use spread out and have at each other curiously and lasciviously, twitching in the random fornication of distraction.

These kettles that wander around boiling, these pestles that get ideas, and the idle funnels that insert themselves into holes for their pleasure. And there too, cast up by the jealous nothingness, are limbs and parts of limbs, and faces that vomit warm into them, and bubbling behinds that do them the favor.

And the saint crouches down and shrinks back; but in his eyes there was still a glance that considered that this was possible: he had seen it. And already his senses are beaten down from the bright resolution of his soul. Already the leaves of his prayer are falling and sticking out of his mouth like a wilted bouquet. His heart has fallen down and flowed out into melancholy. His scourge strikes him weakly, like a tail chasing away flies. His sex is again only in one place, and if a woman comes upright through the slovenly crowd, her open bosom full of breasts, it points at her like a finger.

There were times when I considered these paintings old-fashioned. Not that I had any doubts about them. I could imagine this happening to saints in those days, the zealous, precipitous ones who wanted to begin with God right away at any price. We no longer expect this of ourselves. We suspect that He is too heavy for us, that we have to put Him off in order to do the slow work that separates us from Him. But now I know that this work is just as contested as sainthood; that it arises around everyone who is lonely for the sake of this work, as it formed around the lonely ones of God in their caves and their empty sanctuaries, long ago.

When one speaks of lonely people one always assumes too much. One thinks people know what it's about. No, they don't know. They have never seen a lonely person, they have only hated him without knowing him. They have been his neighbors who used him up, and the voices tempting him from the next room. They have stirred up things against him so that they made loud noises and drowned him out. When he was tender and a child, children banded together against him, and at every stage of his growth he grew against adults. They tracked him down in his lair like an animal to be hunted, and his long youth knew no surcease. And when he did not let himself be worn down, and escaped, they screamed about what emanated from him and called it ugly and suspected it. And when he didn't listen to them they became clearer, and ate up his food and exhaled his air and spat into his poverty so that it became repulsive to him. They brought disrepute upon him as upon someone infectious, and threw stones at him so he would go away more quickly. And they were right in their ancient instinct: for he really was their enemy.

But then, when he did not look up, they bethought themselves. They suspected that with all this they were doing his will, that they were strengthening him in his isolation and helping him to cut himself off from them forever. And so they changed course and applied the final, most extreme, alternative resistance: fame. And at this blaring noise almost everyone looked up and was distracted.

Last night I happened to think of the small green book that I must once have had as a boy; I don't know why I imagine that it came from Mathilde Brahe. When I got it it didn't interest me, and I read it several years later, I believe during a vacation at Ulsgaard. But it was important to me from the very first. It was full of connection through and through, even seen from the outside. The green of the binding signified something, and one immediately recognized that inside it had to be as it was. As if it had been arranged deliberately, first came this smooth, white-on-white watered endpaper, and then the title page that struck one as mysterious. It looked as if there might well have been pictures inside, but there were none, and one had to concede, almost against one's will, that that too was as it should be. What somehow made up for this was finding at a particular place the narrow ribbon of the bookmark which, worn and a little oblique, touching in its confidence that it was still pink, had lain since God knows when between the same two pages. Perhaps it had never been used, and the bookbinder had tipped it in quickly and diligently without really looking. But possibly it was no accident. It could be that someone stopped reading at that place who never read again, that at that moment fate knocked at his door to preoccupy him, that he ended up far from all books, which after all are not life. There was no way of knowing whether the book had been read in further. One could also imagine that it was simply a matter of its having been opened at this place again and again, and that that was what had happened, even if sometimes late in the night. In any event, I felt a shyness at these two pages, as at a mirror one is standing in front of. I never read them. I have no idea whether I read the whole book. It was not very thick, but there were a lot of stories in it, especially in the afternoon, when there was always a story one did not yet know.

I only remember two. I will say which: the end of Grisha Otrepioff and the downfall of Charles the Bold.

God knows whether it impressed me then. But now, after so many years, I remember the description of how the corpse of the false Czar was thrown on the heap with all the others and lay there for three days, torn and stabbed and with a mask in front of his face. There is of course no prospect of the little book ever coming into my hands again. But this passage must have been remarkable. I would also have wanted to read again how his meeting with his mother went. He might have felt himself quite secure, since he had summoned her to Moscow; I am even convinced that at that time he believed in himself so strongly that he actually thought to have his mother summoned to him. And this Marie Nagoi, who came in rapid day-trips from her poor convent, won everything when she agreed to come. But whether his insecurity did not begin just when she recognized him? I am not disinclined to believe that the power of his transformation resided in his no longer being anyone's son.

(That is, finally, the power of all young people who have left home.)[18]

The populace that had wished for him, without imagining a particular person, made him still freer and more unconstrained in his possibilities. But his mother's statement, even as deliberate deceit, still had the power to diminish him. She plucked him out of the fullness of his self-invention; she limited him to a will-less imitation; she reduced him to the one person that he was not: she made him a deceiver. And now this Marina Mniczek entered, breaking him down more gently, denying him in her fashion in that, as came out later, she believed not in him but in everyone. Of course I cannot vouch for how far all that was brought into the story. That, it seems to me, is something that would have had to be narrated.

But even aside from that, this event has not grown old. One could now imagine a narrator who took great pains with the final moments; he would not be wrong. A great many things are going on: how from deepest sleep he jumps to the window and through it and out into the courtyard between the guards. He can't get up by himself; they have to help him. He has probably broken his foot. Leaning on two of the men, he feels that they believe in him. He looks around; the others too believe in him. They almost feel sorry for him,

---

18   Written in the margin of the manuscript (Rilke's note).

these giant Strelitzers, it must come from far back: they knew Ivan Grosny in all his reality, and now believe in him. He would have wanted to enlighten them, but to open his mouth would simply have meant to scream. The pain in his foot is raging, and he is so little conscious of himself at this moment that he knows nothing but the pain. And then there is no time. They are pressing forward, he sees Shuisky and behind him everyone. It will be over quickly. But then his guards close ranks. They will not surrender him. And a miracle occurs. The belief of these old men takes root, suddenly no one any longer dares to move forward. Shuisky, close in front of him, calls in desperation up to a window. The false Czar doesn't look around. He knows who is standing there; he understands that silence will fall, a silence without transition. Now the voice will come that he knows from before; the high, false voice overexerting itself. And then he hears the Czar-Mother denying him.

Up to this point the story tells itself, but now, please, a narrator, a narrator: because from the few lines that remain there must emerge a power that transcends all contradiction. Whether it is said or not, one must swear to it that between voice and pistol shot, infinitely compressed, there was once more will and power in him to be everything. Otherwise one does not understand how brilliantly consistent it is that they bored through his nightdress and stabbed around in him to see if they would hit against the hardness of a person. And that in death he still wore for three days the mask that he had almost already renounced.

When I think back on it now, it seems strange that in the same book the end is told of him who his whole life long was one and the same, like a rock of granite hard and not to be altered, and increasingly heavier on all who bore him. There is a portrait of him in Dijon. But one knows from other sources that he was short, disputatious, defiant, and despairing. It was only his hands that one perhaps would not have thought of. They are angrily warm hands that are continually trying to cool themselves and that involuntarily place themselves on cold things, outspread, with air between all the fingers. Blood could shoot into these hands as it rises to one's head, and when they were clenched they were like the heads of madmen, raging with ideas.

It took unbelievable cautiousness to live with this blood. The duke was locked up in himself with it, and at times he feared it, when it circled around him, dark and intimidating. It could be horribly alien to him, this nimble, half-Portuguese blood that he hardly knew. He was often frightened that it might fall upon him in his sleep and tear him to pieces. He acted as if he had control over it, but he always lived in fear of it. He never dared love a woman for fear his blood might become jealous, and it was so rapacious that wine never touched his lips; instead of drinking he appeased it with rose-jelly. But once he did drink, in the encampment at Lausanne, when Granson was lost; there he was ill and isolated and drank a good deal of unwatered wine. But at that time his blood was sleeping. In his mad last years it often fell into his heavy, animal sleep. Then it showed how much it had him in its power, for when it slept he was nothing. Then no one of his court could enter; he did not understand what they were saying. Wasted as he was, he could not show himself to foreign ambassadors. Then he sat and waited for his blood to wake up. And mostly it exploded with a leap, surged out of his heart, and roared.

For this blood he dragged around all the things that meant nothing to him. The three large diamonds and all the precious stones, the lace of Flanders and the Arras tapestries, in heaps. His silk tent with its stays of woven gold, and four hundred tents for his retinue. And pictures painted on wood, and the twelve apostles of pure silver. And the princes of Tarento and the Duke of Cleves and Philip of Baden and the Lord of Château-Guyon. For he wanted to make his blood believe that he was emperor and there was nothing above him, so that it would fear him. But in spite of such proofs his blood did not believe him; it was a mistrustful blood. Perhaps he kept it in uncertainty for a while. But the horns of Uri betrayed him. After that his blood knew that it was in a lost soul: and wanted out.

That's how I see it now, but what impressed me most then was reading about the day of Epiphany, when they went looking for him.

The young Lothringian prince who, the day before, had ridden into his suffering city of Nancy immediately after the remarkably quick battle, awakened his attendants quite early and asked after the duke. Messenger after messenger was sent out, and the prince himself appeared from time to time at the window, restless and concerned. He did not always recognize who it was they were bringing in on their carts and litters, he only saw that it was not the duke. Nor was he among the wounded, and none of the prisoners who were continually being brought in had seen him. But the refugees brought reports from all sides, and were confused and frightened, as if they feared running into him. It was already growing dark, and there had been no news of him. In the long winter evening the tidings that he had disappeared had time to spread about. And wherever they reached they produced in everyone a violent, overwhelming conviction that he was alive. The duke had perhaps never been as real in everyone's imagination as he was on this night. There was not a house in which people were not watching and waiting for him and imagining his knock. And if he did not come, it was because he had already gone on by.

It froze that night, and it was as if the idea that he was alive froze too, so solid had it become. Years and years passed before it faded. All these people, without rightly knowing it, now insisted on him. The destiny that he had brought upon them was only bearable through his person. It had been so hard for them to learn that he *was*; but now that they knew him they found it was good to remember him and not to forget.

But the next morning, the seventh of January, a Tuesday, the search resumed. And this time it had a leader. It was one of the duke's pages, and it was said that from afar he had seen his master fall; now he was going to point out the place. He himself had told nothing, the Duke of Campobasso had brought him and spoken for him. Now he went on ahead, and the others kept close behind him. Whoever saw this page, muffled up and oddly uncertain, would have had difficulty believing it was really Gian-Battista Colonna, pretty as a girl and with narrow wrists. He was trembling with the cold; the air was stiff with nightfrost, it echoed underfoot like the grinding of teeth. They were all freezing. Only the duke's fool, nicknamed Louis-Onze, was jumping around. He played the dog, ran ahead, came back, and trotted on all fours for a while beside the boy; but wherever he saw a corpse in the distance he sprang over to it and bowed and spoke to it, saying that it should pull itself together and be the one they were seeking. He left it a little time for reflection, but then came back grumpily to the others, threatening and cursing and complaining about the egotism and laziness of the dead. And they kept on and there was no end to it. The town was hardly to be seen any more, for the weather had in the meantime closed in, in spite of the cold, and had become gray and opaque. The countryside lay flat and inert, and the small, compact group appeared more and more lost the further on it went. No one spoke, only an old woman who had come along with them was mouthing something and shaking her head the while; perhaps she was praying.

Suddenly the person in front stopped and looked around. Then he turned abruptly to Lupi, the duke's Portuguese doctor, and pointed ahead. A few steps further on there was a surface of ice, a sort of depression or pool, and in it lay, half submerged, ten or twelve corpses. They had been almost completely stripped and robbed. Lupi walked bent over and attentively from one to the next. And now, as the party spread out one by one, they recognized Olivier de la Marche and the priest. But the old woman was already kneeling in the snow and whimpering, bent over a large hand whose spread-out fingers were staring up at her. They all hastened over. Lupi, with a few servants, tried to turn the corpse over, for it was lying face down. But the face had frozen stiff, and as they pulled it out of the ice one cheek peeled off, thin and brittle, and it appeared that the other had been torn out by dogs or wolves; and the whole face had been sundered by a great wound that began at the ear, so that there could be no talk of a face.

One after another they looked around; everyone thought they would find the Roman right behind them. But they only saw the fool, who came running up angry and bloody. He was holding a cloak in front of him and shaking it, as if something were supposed to fall out; but the cloak was empty. They looked for distinguishing features, and found several. They had lit a fire, and washed the corpse with warm water and wine. The scar on the neck appeared and the places of the two large abscesses. The doctor was no longer in doubt. But there were other signs. A few steps beyond, Louis-Onze had found the corpse of the big black horse Moreau that the duke had ridden out from Nancy that day. He had sat on his mount and let his short legs dangle. The blood was still running from his nose into his mouth, and it was obvious that he enjoyed the taste. One of the servants remembered that a toenail on the duke's left foot was ingrown; now they all looked for it. But the fool wriggled as if he was being tickled and shouted: "Oh Monseigneur, forgive them for revealing your rude secret, the idiots, and for not recognizing you by my long face, in which your virtues reside."

(The duke's fool was also the first to come in when the corpse was laid out. It was in the house of a certain George Marquis, no one could say why. The bier cloth had not yet been laid over him, and so the fool took it all in. The white of the shirt and the scarlet of the cloak stood in sharp and unfriendly contrast between the two blacks of baldachin and bier. In front, scarlet riding boots with large, gilded spurs stood opposite. And that there was a head on top could not be a matter for argument as soon as one saw the crown. It was a large ducal crown with some sort of precious stones. Louis-Onze walked around and examined everything closely. He even felt the satin, although he knew little about it. It might have been good satin, perhaps a little cheap for the House of Burgundy. He stepped back once more to see it all. The colors clashed oddly in the light from the snow. He memorized every single one. "Well-clothed," he finally said in acknowledgment, "perhaps a trace too obvious." Death seemed to him like a puppet master who quickly needs a duke.)[19]

One does well, with certain things that will no longer change, simply to attest to them without regretting or even judging the facts. So it has become clear to me that I was never a proper reader. In child-

---

19   Written in the margin of the manuscript (Rilke's note).

hood, reading seemed to me like a profession that one would take upon oneself at some later time, when all the professions came, one after the other. I had, to be truthful, no distinct idea when that might be. I relied on noticing it when life so to speak reversed and came only from outside, as it earlier came from within. I imagined that this would be clear and obvious and not to be misunderstood. By no means simple: on the contrary quite demanding, complicated, and difficult no doubt, but in any case visible. The peculiar unbound-edness of childhood, its special quality, the never-quite-foreseeable, would then have been overcome. To be sure it was not clear how. Ba-sically it would go on increasing and close itself off on all sides, and the more one looked outside, the more inner things one stirred up in oneself: God knows where it came from. But apparently it grew to an extreme and then suddenly broke off all at once. It was easy to ob-serve that grownups were bothered very little by it; they went about and judged and acted, and if they were ever in difficulties it was due to outward circumstances.

I also put reading along with the beginning of such changes. Then one would go around with books as with acquaintances, there would be time for it, a specific, regular, and pleasantly passing time, just so much as one found agreeable. Of course certain books would be closer to one, but it is not to say that one would be safe from having to lose half an hour away from them here and there: a walk, a rendezvous, the beginning in the theater, or an urgent letter. But that one's hair would be tousled and mussed as if one had lain on it, that one got burning ears and hands cold as metal, that a tall candle burned down beside one and into the candlestick, that would, thank God, be completely excluded.

I bring up these phenomena because I experienced them in my-self, rather accidentally, when I so suddenly got into reading during those vacations at Ulsgaard. It immediately became apparent that I could not do it. I had, to be sure, begun too early, before the time I had projected for it. But that year in Sorö among none but others of about my own age had made me mistrustful of such calculations. Rapid, unexpected experiences had come upon me, and it was clear to see that these experiences were treating me as an adult. They were life-size, which made them as heavy as they were. But in the same measure as I understood their reality, my eyes were also opened to the infinite reality of my being a child. I knew that it would not cease, as little as the other was just beginning. I said to myself that of course everyone was free to make cutoff points, but they were invented. And it turned out that I was too unskilled to think up any for myself. Whenever I tried, life gave me to understand that it knew nothing of them. But if I insisted that my childhood was over, in the same instant everything that was to come vanished, and what remained was exactly as much as a lead soldier has under him to keep him upright.

This discovery understandably isolated me even more. It absorbed me and filled me with a sort of ultimate cheerfulness, which I took for worry because it was far beyond my age. It also unsettled me, as I recall, that since nothing was planned for a specific period of time there were many things I might miss. And when I returned to Ulsgaard in this frame of mind and saw all the books, I fell upon them; in considerable haste, almost with a bad conscience. What I later felt so often I somehow then suspected in advance: that one did not have the right to open one book without committing oneself to read them all. With every line one was cracking open the world. Before the books, and perhaps again after them, the world was whole. But how was I, who could not read, to deal with all of them? There they stood, even in this modest library, in such hopeless numbers, huddled together. I rushed defiantly and in despair from one book to another, charging through the pages like someone who has something special to accomplish. At that time I read Schiller and Baggesen, Öhlenschläger and Schack-Staffeldt, whatever was there of Walter Scott, and Calderon. Many things came into my hands that, so to speak, ought to have been read already, for other things it was much too soon; nothing at that time was just right for the present. But nevertheless I read.

In later years it sometimes happened that I woke up in the night, and the stars were standing there so real and advancing so meaningfully, and I could not understand how one could bring oneself to miss so much world. It was like that, I believe, that I felt whenever I glanced up from the books and looked outside, where it was summer, where Abelone was calling. It always happened unexpectedly for us that she had to call and that I didn't even answer. It was in the midst of our most blissful time. But once reading got hold of me I stuck to it obstinately and, self-important and stubborn, hid myself away from our daily celebrations. Unskilled as I was in taking advantage of the many, often unobtrusive opportunities for a natural happiness, I was not reluctant to promise myself future reconciliations arising from the growing rift, reconciliations that were more beckoning the further off one put them.

Moreover, my reading-sleep ended one day as suddenly as it had begun, and then we had an angry falling out. For Abelone spared me no ridicule or superciliousness, and whenever I met her in the arbor she claimed she was reading. On that particular Sunday morning the book lay closed beside her, but she seemed more than sufficiently occupied with the currants, which she was carefully stroking from their small clusters with a fork.

It must have been one of those early mornings that there are in

July, fresh, rested hours in which everywhere something cheerful and spontaneous is happening. Millions of small, irrepressible motions form a mosaic of the most convinced existence; things swing into each other and out into the air, and their coolness makes the shadows clear and the sun a soft, spiritual gleam. In the garden there is no one chief thing; everything is everywhere, and one would have to be in everything in order not to miss anything.

The wholeness was repeated in Abelone's small actions. It had been such a happy idea to be doing just that, and just the way she did it. Her hands, bright in the shade, worked so easily and harmoniously together, and the round berries sprang so purposefully from the fork into the bowl lined with dew-hazed grape leaves, where other berries were already heaped up, stippled red and blond, with healthy seeds in their tart interior. Under these circumstances I could ask for nothing better than to look on, but since it was apparent that this would be refused, in order to appear casual I seized the book, sat down on the opposite side of the table and, without paging through it for long, immersed myself in it at random.

"If you would at least read it aloud, bookworm!" Abelone said after a while. That no longer sounded nearly so quarrelsome, and since in my opinion it was high time that we made up, I immediately read aloud, straight on up to a certain section and then the next heading: To Bettina.[20]

"No, not the answers," Abelone interrupted me, and suddenly put down the small fork as if she were exhausted. Immediately thereafter she laughed at the face with which I was looking at her.

"My God, how badly you read that, Malte."

Then I had to admit that I had not been paying attention to it for

---

20   Bettina von Arnim, *Goethe's Correspondence with a Child* (1835).

a single moment. "I was only reading so you would interrupt me," I confessed, turning red, and paged back to the title of the book. Now I saw for the first time what it was. "Why not the answers?" I asked, curious.

It was as if Abelone had not heard me. She was sitting there in her bright dress as if everywhere within she were growing as dark as her eyes had become.

"Hand it over," she said suddenly as if angry, took the book from my hand, and opened it to just where she wanted. And then she read one of Bettina's letters.

I don't know how much of it I understood, but it was as if I were being solemnly promised that at some time I would understand it all. And while her voice grew and finally almost resembled the voice I knew from her singing, I was ashamed that I had imagined our reconciliation so pettily. For I certainly understood that this was what it was. But now it was happening somewhere in greatness, far above me, where I could not reach.

The promise is still fulfilling itself. At some point this same book showed up among my books, the few from which I do not part. Now it falls open for me too at the places I happen to be thinking of, and when I read it is unclear whether I am thinking of Bettina or of Abelone. No, Bettina has become more real in me; Abelone, whom I knew, was like a preparation for her, and now she has blended into Bettina in me as in her own spontaneous being. For through all her letters this marvelous Bettina has created space, the most spacious form. From the very beginning she spread herself out as broadly as if she were writing after her death. Everywhere she placed herself deeply into being, as part of it, and whatever happened to her was eternally part of nature; there she recognized herself and crystallized herself out of it almost painfully, guessing her way back with effort from old documents, conjuring herself like a ghost, and enduring.

You *were* just now, Bettina, I recognize you. Is not the earth still warm from you, and the birds still leave room for your voice. The dew is different, but the stars are still the stars of your nights. Or is not the world altogether your creation? For how often have you set it on fire with your love and seen it blaze and flare up, and secretly substituted for it another world, when all were sleeping. You felt yourself so fully in harmony with God, when every morning you desired of Him a new world in which all the people He had made could enter. It seemed paltry to you to care for and improve them, you consumed them and held out your hands for ever more world. For your love could cope with everything.

How is it possible that everyone is not still telling of your love? What has happened that was more remarkable since? With what, then, are they busying themselves? You yourself knew the value of your love, you said it aloud to your greatest poet so that he would make it human; for it still belonged to the elements. But he talked people out of it when he wrote you. Everyone has read those answers and believes them more, because the poet is clearer to them than nature. But perhaps it will one day be seen that this was the limit of his greatness. This loving person was a responsibility laid upon him, and he did not rise to it. What does it mean that he was not able to respond? Such love needs no response, it contains summons and answer in itself; it listens to itself. But he would have had to humble himself before this love in all his finery and write what it dictated, with both hands, like John on Patmos, kneeling. There was no choice in the face of this voice that "performed the office of angels," that had come to envelop him and remove him to the eternal. There stood the wagon for his fiery ascension. There he left empty the dark myth prepared for his death.

Fate loves to invent patterns and figures. Its difficulty resides in complexity. But life is difficult from simplicity. It contains only a few things not of human measure. The saint, by rejecting fate, chooses these things in the sight of God. But that in accord with her nature woman must make the same choice in relation to man conjures up the fatefulness of all love relationships: resolute and without fate, like an eternal presence, she stands beside him who transforms himself. The loving woman always exceeds the beloved man, because life is greater than fate. Her devotion wants to be immeasurable: this is her happiness. But the nameless suffering of her life has always been this, that it is asked of her to limit this devotion.

No other lament has ever been lamented by women: Heloise's first two letters contain only them, and five hundred years later they emerge again from the letters of the Portuguese nun; one recognizes them again like a bird's cry. And suddenly there goes through the bright space the insight of this nun, this figure at the furthest remove from Sappho: an insight the centuries did not find because they were seeking it in fate.

I have never dared buy a newspaper from him. I'm not sure that he always carries several as he slowly shuffles along back and forth outside the Luxembourg Gardens all evening long. He turns his back to the fence, and his hand keeps brushing the stone base on which the bars stand upright. He so flattens himself that many people pass by every day without ever seeing him. Of course he still has the remnants of a voice and calls out to them; but it is no different from a noise in a lamp or an oven, or the noise of water in a grotto that drips at odd intervals. And the world is so arranged that there are people who their whole lives long pass by in the interval, when he, more soundless than anything active, moves on like a clock's hand, like the shadow of one, like time.

How wrong I was to look reluctantly. I'm ashamed to write down that often, when I was near him, I adopted the pace of others, as if I wasn't aware of him. Then I heard it say in him: "La Presse," and again immediately afterwards, and a third time at rapid intervals. And the people beside me looked around, looking for the voice. I alone acted as if I were in a greater hurry than anyone, as if I had noticed nothing, as if I were totally preoccupied with my thoughts.

And in truth I was. I was preoccupied with how to represent him, I undertook the task of imagining him, and sweat broke out from the strain. For I had to make him the way one makes a dead person, for whom there is no longer any evidence, no constituent elements; who is to be accomplished absolutely and totally inwardly. I know now that it helped a little to think of all the dismounted Christ figures of streaky ivory that lie around in every curio shop. The thought of some pietà came and went: all this apparently only to evoke a certain angle at which he was holding his long face, and the miserable stubble of beard in the shadows of his cheeks, and the final painful blindness of his inscrutable expression, which was directed diagonally upwards. But beside that there was so much that was part of him; for this I understood already at that time, that nothing about him was incidental: not the way the coat, standing out in back, made his collar visible all around, this low collar that surrounded the gullies of his neck in a great curve without touching it; not the greenish-black tie that was fastened far outside it all; and most especially not the hat, an old, stiff, high felt hat, which he wore the way all blind people wear their hats: without connection to the lines of his face, without the possibility of his face adding anything and creating a new external unity; wearing it no differently from any other normal, alien object. In my cowardice at not looking at him I went so far that the image of this man, often without reason, strongly and painfully crystallized in me to such intense misery that, oppressed by it, I resolved to counter and dispose of it through the picture's growing completeness in my imagination by concentrating on the outward facts. It was toward evening. I undertook to walk past him immediately, paying attention.

One must know that it was getting on toward spring. The wind of the day had died down, the alleys were long and satisfied; where they ended houses shimmered, new as fresh fractures in some white metal. But it was a metal that surprised by its lightness. In the broad, receding streets crowds of people were mingling, almost without fearing the vehicles, which were few. It must have been Sunday. The towers of Saint-Sulpice were cheerful and unexpectedly high in the complete calm, and one involuntarily looked out through the narrow, almost Roman alleys into the season. In the Garden and in front of it so many people were moving back and forth that I did not see him right away. Or was it that at first I did not recognize him through the crowd?

I knew immediately that my mental picture was worthless. The devotion of his misery, unmediated by any circumspection or pretence, exceeded my means. I had grasped neither the angle of inclination of his attitude nor the horror with which the inner side of his eyelids continually seemed to be filling him. I had never thought of his mouth, which was drawn in like the opening of a gutter. It's possible he had memories; but now nothing was any longer added to his soul beyond the daily amorphous feeling of the stone edge behind him on which his hand was wearing itself out. I had stopped, and while I took all this in almost simultaneously, I felt that he was wearing a different hat and, without doubt, a Sunday necktie; it had a diagonal pattern of yellow and violet squares, and as for the hat, it was a cheap new straw hat with a green band. These colors are of course not in the least important, and it is fussy of me to have retained them. I only mean that they were on him like the softest part of a bird's underside. He himself got no pleasure from it, and who among all these people (I looked around) would imagine that this finery was for his sake?

My God, it suddenly occurred to me fiercely. *This* is the way you really are. There are proofs of your existence. I have forgotten them all and never ever desired one, for what monstrous obligation would lie in their certainty. And yet now it is being revealed to me. This is your taste, here you find pleasure. If we would only learn above all to endure and not judge. What are the difficult things? What the merciful ones? You alone know.

When it is winter again and I have to have a new coat—grant me that I wear it *this* way, as long as it is new.

It's not that I want to differentiate myself from them when I go around in better clothes that have been mine from the beginning, and insist on living somewhere. I haven't got as far as they have. I don't have the heart for their life. If my arm should wither, I think I would hide it. But she (I don't know who she was at other times) appeared every day before the terraces of the cafés, and although it was quite difficult for her to take off her coat and get herself out of her indistinct outer and inner garments she spared no effort, and took things off, undressing for so long that one could hardly expect there to be any more. And then she stood before us, modestly, in her stunted, withered play, and it was a rare sight.

No, it's not that I want to differentiate myself from them; but I would be arrogant if I wanted to be their equal. I am not. I would have neither their strength nor their measure. I nourish myself, and so exist from meal to meal, completely without mystery; but they maintain themselves almost like eternal beings. They stand on their daily corners, even in November, and don't complain about winter. The fog comes and blurs their outlines and makes them uncertain: they stay the same. I was away, I was sick, I missed a great deal: but they, however, have not died.

(I don't even know how it is possible for schoolchildren to stand up in rooms full of gray-smelling cold; who strengthens them, the hurried little skeletons, so that they run out into the grown-up city, into the murky lees of the night, into the everlasting schoolday, always still small, always filled with anticipation, always late. I have no notion of the amount of assistance that is continually consumed.)[21]

This city is full of such people, who slowly slide down to their level. Most resist at first; but then there are these faded, aging girls, who continually allow themselves to pass away without resistance, strong, unused in their essence, girls who have never been loved.

Perhaps, O my God, you think that I should drop everything and love them. Or why is it so hard for me not to go after them when they overtake me? Why do I suddenly invent the sweetest, most nocturnal words, and why is my voice soft in me between throat and heart? Why do I imagine how I would hold them in my breath with un-

---

21   Written in the margin of the manuscript (Rilke's note).

speakable caution, these dolls with whom life has played, spreading out their arms spring after spring for nothing, nothing at all, until they became loose in the shoulders? They have never fallen from a high hope and so they are not broken; but they are exhausted and already too unfit for life. Only lost cats come to them in their rooms in the evening and secretly scratch them and sleep on them. Sometimes I follow one of these women past two alleys. They slink along the houses, people are continually going by, concealing them, further on these women vanish behind the others as if they were nothing.

And yet I know that if someone tried to be fond of them they would lean heavily on him, like people who have walked too far who stop walking. I believe that only Jesus could bear them, only he still has resurrection in all his limbs; but nothing about them interests him. Only lovers seduce him, not those who wait for the beloved with a small talent, as with a cold lamp.

I know that if I am destined for the highest things it will not help to disguise myself in my better clothes. Did not he in the midst of his kingdom fall below the lowest? Instead of rising up he sank down to the ground. It is true, at times I believed in the other kings, although the parks no longer show any evidence of them. But it is night, it is winter, I'm freezing, I believe in him. For glory lasts only a moment, and we have never seen anything that is longer than misery. But the king should endure.

Is this king not the only one who maintained himself in his madness like wax flowers in a glass case? In the churches they prayed for a long life for the others, but the chancellor Jean Charlier Gerson wanted this king to be eternal, and that was at the time when he was already the neediest one, wretched and of extreme poverty despite his crown.

That was when strange men with blackened faces fell upon him in his bed from time to time in order to tear off him the rotted, festering shirt that he had for so long kept for himself. The room was darkened, and they tore off the rotten tatters from under his stiff shoulders wherever they could grab hold of them. Then one of them shone a light, and only then did they discover the festering wound in his chest into which the iron amulet had sunk because every night he had pressed it into himself with all the power of his zeal; now it lay deep within him, fearfully precious, in a pearly hem of pus, like miracle-bringing remains in the hollow of a reliquary. They had sought out hard-bitten laborers, but these men were not immune from nausea when the worms, disturbed, reached out toward them from the Flanders nightshirt, and, falling out of the folds, pulled themselves up here and there on their sleeves. There was no doubt things had gotten worse with him since the days of the parva regina; for she at least had still wanted to lie with him, young and lucid as she was. Then she had died. And now no one any longer dared bed a concubine with this carrion. She had not left behind the words and the tendernesses with which the king was to be eased. So no one any longer penetrated his mind's reversion to rankness; no one helped him up out of the ravines of his soul; no one understood when he himself suddenly climbed out with the round glance of an animal pacing on the meadow. If he then recognized the preoccupied face of Juvenal des Ursins, he thought of the empire as it had been at the last. And he wanted to make up what he had lost.

But it lay in the events of those times that they were not to be easily encompassed. Where something happened it happened with all its weight, and was cut as if from a single piece, as one said. Or what was to be deduced from the murder of his brother that yesterday Valentina Visconti, whom he had always called his dear sister, had knelt before him raising nothing but lamentations and accusations from her widow's black? And today there stood before him for hours a tough, talkative lawyer who affirmed the right of the princely murderer until the crime faded to transparency and as if it wanted to fly brightly up to heaven. And to be righteous meant saying that everyone was right; for Valentina d'Orléans died grieving, although she had been promised revenge. And what good was it pardoning the Burgundian duke again and again; the dark rutting of despair had come over him, so that for weeks he had been living in a tent in the forest of Argilly, maintaining that at night he had to listen to the screams of the deer to find relief.

If one had thought all that over, again and again to the end, short as it was, the people desired to see one person and they saw one person: baffled. But the people were happy at the sight; they understood that this was the king: this silent, patient man who was only there to sanction that God act over his head in His late impatience. In these enlightened moments on the balcony of his Hôtel de Saint-Pol the king perhaps had an intimation of his secret progress. He thought of the day at Roosbecke, when his uncle de Berry had taken him by the hand to lead him before his first achieved victory; on that remarkably long November day he had looked over the mass of the Ghentians, who had strangled themselves from tying themselves together so tightly, ridden against from all sides. Intertwined with one another like a monstrous brain they lay in the heaps into which they had tied themselves in order to be packed in tightly. It took one's breath away to see the suffocated faces here and there; one could not help imagining that they had been forced up far above the crowded, still-standing corpses by the sudden exit of so many desperate souls.

This had been inculcated in him as the beginning of his fame. And he had retained it. But, if that had formerly been the triumph of death, this triumph was that he was standing here on his weak knees, upright before all these eyes: the mystery of love. He had seen with the former triumph that one could understand that battlefield, terrible as it was. This now before him did not want to be understood; it was just as miraculous as the stag with the golden neckband had been in the forest of Senlis. Except that now he himself was the phenomenon, and others were absorbed in looking at him. And he did not doubt that they were breathless and had the same broad expectation of the kind that had overcome him on that youthful hunting day when the silent face eyeing him questioningly stepped out from the underbrush. The mystery of his visibility spread over his gentle figure; he did not stir for fear of perishing; the thin smile on his broad, simple face assumed a natural duration like that of stone saints, and cost him no effort. So he offered himself, and it was one of those moments that are eternity, seen abbreviated. The crowd could hardly bear it. Strengthened, fed by an inexhaustibly growing comforting, its loud shout of joy broke through the silence. But only Juvenal des Ursins was left up there on the balcony, and he called out into the next period of calm that the king would be coming down the rue Saint-Denis to the Passion Brotherhood, to see the cult of the mysteries.

For such days the king was full of gentle consciousness. If a painter of that time had sought a clue for existence in paradise, he would have found no more perfect model than the stilled figure of the king as it stood under the fall of his shoulders in one of the high windows of the Louvre. The king was leafing through the small book of Christine de Pisan called "The Path of Long Learning," which had been dedicated to him. He was not reading the learned polemics of that allegorical parliament that had set as its task finding the prince worthy of reigning over the world. The book always fell open for him at the simplest places: where the heart was spoken of that for thirteen years had served only as a retort over flames of pain to distill the water of bitterness for the eyes; he understood that true consolation only began when happiness had been long enough over and was forever past. Nothing meant more to him than this consolation. And while his glance appeared to be taking in the bridge over there, he loved to see the world, the past world, through this heart that was moved to distant views by the strong sibyl: the risky seas, cities with strange towers, kept closed by the proof of distances; the ecstatic solitude of gathered mountain chains and the sky scanned in furrowed doubt, a sky that gradually grew closed like an infant's skull.

But when someone entered he shrank back, and his mind slowly misted over. He allowed himself to be led away from the window and given things to do. They had imparted to him the habit of tarrying for hours over illustrations, and he was satisfied, but it irritated him that in paging through them one never had several pictures before one at the same time but that they sat firmly in the folios so they could not be moved about. Then someone remembered the cards of a game that had been completely forgotten, and the king favored him who brought it, so much after his heart were these cards that were colorful and could be moved around singly and were full of figuration. And while card games came into fashion among the courtiers, the king sat in his library and played alone. Just as he now turned up two kings side by side, so had God recently placed him and the Emperor Wenzel together; sometimes a queen died, then he laid an ace of hearts on her, it was like a tombstone. He was not surprised that in this game there were several popes; he put Rome over there at the edge of the table, and this one, under his right hand, was Avignon. He was indifferent to Rome, for some reason he imagined it to be round and paid it no further attention. But Avignon he knew. And hardly had he thought it than his memory recalled the lofty, hermetic palace and overstrained itself. He closed his eyes and had to breathe in deeply. He was afraid he would have bad dreams in the coming night.

But on the whole it was really a calming pastime, and they were right to keep bringing him back to it again and again. Such hours confirmed him in the view that he was the king, King Charles the Sixth. That does not mean that he overestimated himself; he was far from thinking that he was more than such a card, but the certainty strengthened in him that he too was a specific card, perhaps a bad one, one angrily played that always lost: but always the same one, never a different one. And yet, when a week had passed this way in monotonous self-confirmation, something in him became anxious. The skin tightened over his forehead and neck, as if he were suddenly feeling his too-distinct contour. No one knew to what temptation he was yielding when he then asked about the mysteries, and could not wait for them to begin. And when it had come to this, he lived more in the rue Saint-Denis than in his Hôtel de Saint-Pol.

It was the fatefulness of these pictorial poems that they continually added to themselves and expanded and grew to tens of thousands of lines, so that time in them was finally real time; something as if one were to make a globe on the scale of the earth. The hollow platform under which was hell, over which the scaffolding of a balcony without a railing, jutting from a pillar, signified paradise, only served to diminished the deception. For that century had in fact made heaven and hell earthly: it lived from the energies of both, in order to survive itself.

Those were the days of that Avignon Christianity that a generation before had gathered around John the Twenty-second, with so many involuntary refugees following him that, on the site of his pontificate, the mass of this palace immediately arose, closed in and heavy like an emergency shelter for all the homeless souls. But he himself, the small, light, spiritual old man, still dwelt in the open. While he, hardly arrived, had begun without delay to act rapidly and efficiently in every direction, the dishes spiced with poison were standing on his table; the first beaker always had to be poured out, because the fragment of unicorn was discolored when the taster withdrew it. At a loss where to hide them, the seventy-year-old pope carried around the wax portraits that had been made of him to bring him down; and he scratched himself on the long needles that were stuck through them. The portraits could be melted down. Yet he had already been so horrified by these secret simulacra that, against his strong will, the thought had several times occurred to him that this could be fatal to himself, and that then he would disappear in the fire like the wax. His shrunken body only grew more withered from dread, and more enduring. But now the body of his realm was threatened; from Granada the Jews had been incited to eradicate all Christians, and this time they had secured more fearsome executioners. No one doubted, immediately after the first rumors, that the lepers were about to attack; several people had already seen how they had thrown bundles of their putrid decay into the wells. That people immediately considered this possible was not credulity; on the contrary, the belief had become so strong that it sank out of the hands of those who trembled down to the bottom of the wells. And once again the industrious old man had to keep poison away from his blood. At the time of his fits of superstition he had prescribed the Angelus for himself and those around him against the demons of twilight, and now this calming prayer was rung every evening in the whole agitated world. But otherwise all the bulls and letters that emanated from him resembled a spiced wine more than an herb tea. The Empire had not placed itself under his treatment, but he never tired of overwhelming it with proofs of its illness, and people from the Far East were already turning to this imperious doctor.

But then the incredible happened. He had preached on All Saints' Day, longer and more warmly than usual. In sudden need, as if to see himself again, he had revealed his belief; he had slowly, with all his strength lifted it up out of its eighty-five-year-old tabernacle and displayed it on the chancel: and then they screamed at him. All Europe screamed: this was a bad belief.

Then the Pope vanished. For days no decree went out from him; he was on his knees in his prayer room plumbing the secret of those who act, who injure their souls thereby. Finally he appeared, exhausted from his difficult reflections, and recanted. He recanted again and again. Recanting became the senile passion of his mind. It could happen that he had the cardinals awakened in the night to speak with them of his remorse. And perhaps what ultimately sustained his life beyond all measure was only the hope to humble himself as well before Napoleon Orsini, who hated him and did not want to come.

Jacob de Cahors had recanted. And one might think that God himself had wanted to prove the error of his ways, since so soon after that God had called to Him the son of the Count de Ligny, who only seemed to be waiting for his maturity on earth in order to enter heaven's spiritual sensuality in his manly state. Many of those living remembered this lucid boy as cardinal, and how as a tender youth he had become bishop and died in the ecstasy of his perfection when he was barely eighteen. One encountered those who had been dead: for the air at his grave, in which pure life lay released, had for a long time still its effect on their corpses. But was there not something despairing even in this precocious saintliness? Was it not a wrong done to everyone that the pure fabric of this soul had been saturated as if it were only a question of dyeing it in the pure shining scarlet of the time? Was it not felt as something like a counterattack for this young prince to spring away from the earth in his passionate ascension? Why were not the shining ones tarrying among the toiling candlemakers? Was it not this darkness that had brought John the Twenty-second to assert that there could be no complete blessedness *before* the Last Judgment, nowhere, not even among the blessed? And indeed, how much self-opinionated, dogged determination did it take to imagine that while here such great confusion was going on, somewhere there were coutenances reposing in God's reflection, reclining on angels and pacified by their inexhaustible view of Him.

I sit here in the cold night and write and know all that. Perhaps I know it because of that man I met back when I was little. He was very tall, I even think he must have attracted attention because of his height.

As improbable as it sounds, I had somehow managed to get out of the house alone, toward evening. I ran, went around the corner, and in the same moment ran into him. I don't understand how what then happened could have played out in no more than five seconds. However brief in the telling, it lasts much longer. I had hurt myself running into him; I was small, it seemed brave of me that I didn't cry, and I was also expecting to be comforted. Since he did not do so, I thought he was embarrassed; I suspected that he could not think of the right pleasantry to resolve the matter. I was already cheerful enough to help him with it, but for that it would have been necessary to look into his face. I have said that he was tall. Now he had not, as would have been natural, bent down to me, so that he remained at a height for which I was not prepared. In front of me there was still nothing but the odor and the peculiar hardness of his suit, which I had felt. Suddenly his face appeared. What was it like? I don't know, I don't want to know. It was the face of an enemy. And beside this face, right beside it, at the height of his terrible eyes, was, like a second head, his fist. Even before I had time to turn my head away I was already running; I squirmed by him on the left and ran straight down an empty, dreadful street, the street of an unknown city, of a city in which nothing is forgiven.

At that time I experienced what I now understand: heavy, massive, desperate time. The time in which the kiss of two reconciling lovers was only a sign to the murderers standing around. The lovers drank from the same goblet, in front of everyone's eyes they mounted the same horse, and it was spread around that they would sleep that night in the same bed: but with every contact their repulsion for each other became so urgent that, as often as one saw the beating veins of the other, a morbid nausea surged in him, like the sight of a toad. The time in which a brother fell upon his brother and held him captive on account of the other's greater inheritance; to be sure, the king intervened for the mistreated brother and secured his freedom and his property. Occupied with other, distant destinies, the older brother granted the younger peace, and in letters regretted his wrong. But in spite of all that the freed brother could no longer regain his equilibrium. The century shows him in pilgrim's clothes, wandering from church to church, inventing devotions that became stranger and stranger. Weighed down by amulets, he whispered his fears to the monks of Saint-Denis, and in their registers was long inscribed the hundred-pound wax candle that he had thought it good to dedicate to Saint Louis. He never achieved a life of his own; until his end he felt his brother's envy and anger in distorted constellation over his heart. And Count de Foix, Gaston Phoebus, whom everyone admired, had he not publicly at Lourdes killed his cousin Ernault, the captain of the English king? But what was this straightforward murder against the dreadful accident that he had not put down the sharp nail trimmer when with his famously beautiful hands he had stroked in twitching reproach the bare neck of his sleeping son? The room was dark, they had to bring candles to see the blood that had come down through so many generations and, secretly emerging from the tiny wound of this exhausted boy, now deserted forever a precious lineage.

Who could be strong and refrain from murder? Who in that time did not know that the utmost was unavoidable? Here and there a strange presentiment overcame one whose glance during the day had met the testing glance of his murderer. He withdrew, he locked himself in, he wrote the end of his testament and finally ordered the litter of woven willow, the habit of a Celestine monk, and ashes to be strewn. Strange minstrels appeared before his castle, and he rewarded them royally for their songs, which were at one with the voices of his vague premonitions. When the dogs looked up doubt was in them, and they became less secure in their behavior toward him. From the motto that had prevailed his whole life long a newly revealed second meaning gently emerged. Many habits of long standing seemed out of date, but it was as if no substitute came any longer to replace them. If plans came up, he handled them broadly, talking about them without really believing in them; on the other hand, certain memories took on unexpected finality. In the evening by the fireplace one thought of abandoning oneself to them. But the night outside, which one no longer knew, suddenly became quite loud in one's hearing. The ear, experienced in so many free or dangerous nights, made out individual fragments of the silence.

And yet this time it was different. Not the night between yesterday and today: a night. Night. Beau Sire Dieu, and then the Resurrection. Hardly that in such hours the praising of a beloved intruded: these praisings were all disguised in aubades and poems of service to one's lady, become incomprehensible under long, sumptuous, drawn-out names. At most, in the dark, like the full, feminine, up-lifted gaze of a bastard son.

And then, before the late supper, this pensiveness over the hands in the silver washbasin. One's own hands. Whether a connection could be made with hers? A sequence, a continuation in grasping and releasing? No. Everyone attempted the part and the counterpart. They all canceled each other out, action there was none.

There was no action except by the missionary brothers. The king, having seen how they conducted themselves, drew up a license for them himself. He called them his dear brothers; never had anyone meant so much to him. They were given approval in writing to go around in their significance among the worldly; for the king wished for nothing more than that they would inspire many and spirit them into their strong movement, in which order reigned. As for himself, he longed to learn from them. Did he not, just like them, wear the insignia and clothes of an idea? When he looked at them he could believe that this might be learnt: to come and go, to express oneself and turn away so that there was no doubt. Enormous hopes lay on his heart. In this restlessly lit, peculiarly undefined hall of the Hospital of the Trinity he sat every day in the best place, stood up with excitement, and pulled himself together like a schoolboy. Others wept; but he was filled with shining inner tears and only pressed his cold hands together so he could bear it. Sometimes, at the utmost, when a player left the game of cards and suddenly vanished from his great sight, he raised his face and shrank back: how long had *he* been there: Monseigneur Saint Michaël, up above, who had come forward to the edge of the beams in his mirroring silver armament.

At such moments he sat up straight. He looked around as if a decision were impending. He was quite close to seeing the counterpart to this action: the great, fearful, profane passion in which he was playing a role. But suddenly it was over. Everyone was moving around without purpose. Open torches came toward him, and shapeless shadows cast themselves upward into the vaults. People he did not know were pulling at him. He wanted to act his role: but nothing came out of his mouth, his movements yielded no gestures. People were pressing so oddly around him that the idea came to him that he should be bearing the cross. And he wanted to wait for them to bring it to him. But they were stronger, and slowly pushed him out.

Outside, much has changed. I don't know how. But within and before you, O my God, within before you, we are spectators: are we not without action? We discover that we don't know the role, we look for a mirror, we want to take off our makeup and falseness and be real. But somewhere a piece of disguise that we have forgotten still clings to us. A trace of exaggeration remains in our eyebrows, we don't notice that the corners of our mouth are bent down. And so we walk around, a mockery and a lone half: neither being nor actor.

That was in the amphitheater at Orange. Without really looking up at it, aware only of the rustic fragment that now constitutes its façade, I had entered through the caretaker's small glass door. I found myself among columns lying on the ground and small mallow shrubs, but they hid from me only for a moment the open mussel shell of the spectators' semicircle lying there, divided by the afternoon shadows like a gigantic concave sundial. I quickly went toward it. As I climbed up among the rows I felt how I was shrinking in this setting. Above, somewhat higher, scattered about, a few strangers were standing around in idle curiosity; their clothes were unpleasantly loud, but of a standard not worth mentioning. For a while they stared at me and were surprised at how small I was. That made me turn around.

Oh, I was totally unprepared. There was a play. An immense, superhuman drama was in progress, the drama of this powerful wall of the stage whose vertical divisions appeared triply, resounding with greatness, almost annihilating yet suddenly moderate in excess.

I let myself go in happy consternation. What was rearing up opposite with the face-like arrangement of its shadows, with the gathered darkness in the mouth at its center, bordered above by the even locks of the coiffure of the protruding cornice: this was the strong antique mask that altered everything, behind which the world coalesced into a face. Here, in this great, curved seating space for the spectators there reigned a sucking, expectant, empty existence. All action was on the side facing them: Gods and fate. And from that side there came (if one looked high up), lightly, above the spine of the wall, the eternal entrance of the sky.

That hour, I understand it now, shut me out from our theaters forever. What would I do in them? What should I do presented with a stage in which this wall (the icon wall of Russian churches) has been dismantled because one no longer has the energy to press the action through its hardness, the vaporous action that exudes in heavy, full drops of oil. Now plays tumble in pieces through the coarse crude sieve of the stages and pile up and are carted off, when there are enough of them. It is the same raw reality that lies around in the streets and houses, only that more of it collects in these plays than fits into an evening in the theater.

(Let us be frank, we have no theater, as little as we have a God: for that you need community. Everyone has his own particular ideas and fears, and he reveals to others just enough of them as is useful to him and appropriate. We are continually diluting our understanding so it will cover things, instead of screaming toward the wall a common need behind which the incomprehensible has time to gather and harness itself.)[22]

If we had a theater, would you, tragic one,[23] be standing over and over again so slender, so exposed, so without pretense of form before those who amuse their shallow curiosity with the pain you display? You anticipated, O inexpressibly moving one, the reality of your suffering that time in Verona when you, almost still a child playing theater, held only a spray of roses before your face, like a masking frontal view that was meant to heighten your concealment.

It's true you were the child of actors, and when your family acted they wanted to be seen; but you transcended the mould. For you

---

22   Written in the margin of the manuscript (Rilke's note).

23   Eleanore Duse, the famous actress.

this profession would become what becoming a nun was for Marianna Alcoforado without her suspecting it, a disguise dense and sufficiently enduring behind which to be relentlessly miserable, with
the urgency with which invisible blessed ones are blessed. In all the
cities you came to they described your gestures; but they did not
understand how you, becoming more hopeless every day, again and
again raised up a poem in front of you so that it might hide you. You
held your hair, your hands, any solid thing, in front of the places
shining through. You breathed on those places that were transparent; you made yourself small; you hid yourself the way children hide
themselves, and then you uttered that short, happy outburst, and at
the very least an angel should have been permitted to seek you out.
But when you then cautiously looked up there was no doubt that
they had been seeing you the whole time, everyone in that hollow,
ugly space full of eyes: you, you, you, and nothing else.

And it occurred to you to hold your arm close but extend it out
to them with the finger-sign against the evil eye. It came to you to
tear your face away from them, the face they were feeding on. It came
to you to be yourself. Your fellow-actors lost courage; as if they had
been locked up with a female panther they sidled along the wings
and spoke what they had to, just so as not to provoke you. But you
pulled them forward and set them there and dealt with them as with
something real. The floppy doors, the illusory curtains, the objects
with no back, urged you on to contradiction. You felt how your heart
was incessantly surging to an immense reality and, frightened, you
tried once more to flick the glances off yourself like long threads of
Indian summers. But in their fear of the ultimate they were already
breaking out into applause: as if to deflect from themselves at the last
moment something that would force them to change their lives.

Those who are loved live badly and in danger. Oh, if they could transcend themselves and become lovers. Around lovers there is nothing but security. No one suspects them any longer, and they themselves are not able to betray themselves. In them the secret has become whole, like nightingales they shout it out as oneness, it has no parts. They lament for a person; but all nature joins in: it is the lament for an eternal being. They rush after the lost one but with their first steps are already racing past him, and in front of them is only God. Their legend is that of Byblis, who pursued Caunus all the way to Lycia. The urging of her heart chased her on his traces through all the lands, and finally she reached the end of her strength, but so strong was the agitation of her being that she, sinking down, appeared again beyond death as a spring, quickening, as a quickening spring.

What else happened to the Portuguese nun but that inwardly she became a spring? And to you, Heloïse? And to you, lovers whose lamentations have come down to us: Gaspara Stampa; the Countess of Die and Clara d'Anduze; Louise Labé, Marceline Desbordes, Elisa Mercoeur? But you, poor fugitive Aïssé, you hesitated and yielded. Tired Julie Lespinasse. Melancholy legend of the happy park: Marie-Anne de Clermont.

I still know precisely, once, ages ago, at home, I found a jewel case. It was as big as two hands, in the form of a fan with a recessed flower border in dark green morocco. I opened it: it was empty. After such a long time, now I can say that. But back then, when I had opened it, I saw only of what this emptiness consisted: of velvet, of a small mound of light, no longer fresh velvet; of the empty hollow left by the jewels that, brighter by a trace with melancholy, coursed through it. That could be borne for a moment. But for the ones who stay behind as those who were the objects of love, it is perhaps always thus.

Leaf back in your diaries. Wasn't there always around spring a time in which the year bursting forth affected you girls like a reproach? There was in you the desire to be happy, and yet when you went out into the spacious openness an alienation arose outside in the air and your walking became uncertain, as on a ship. The garden was beginning; but you (that was it), you dragged winter in and the previous year; for you it was at best a continuation. While you waited, hoping your souls would participate, you suddenly felt the weight of your limbs, and something like the possibility of becoming ill intruded on your open anticipation. You ascribed it to your dresses that were too light, you drew the shawls around your shoulders, you ran down the tree-lined walk to the end: then you stood in the wide rondel, your hearts beating, resolved to be one with it all. But a bird sounded and was alone and denied you. Alas, would you have to have died?

Perhaps. Perhaps what is new is that we survive these: the year and love. Flowers and fruits are ripe when they fall; animals feel themselves and find one another and are satisfied. But we, who have made God for ourselves, we can not find satisfaction. We put off our nature, we need more time. What is a year to us? What are all of them? Even before we have begun God we are already praying to Him: let us survive the night. And then being sick. And then love.

That Clémence de Bourges had to die on her upward path. She, who was incomparable; among the instruments that she knew how to play like no one else, the most beautiful one played unforgettably in the least sound of her voice. Her girlhood was of such great resolve that a flooding woman in love could dedicate to this rising heart the book of sonnets in which every line was unslaked. Louise Labé did not fear frightening this child with the travails of love. She showed her the nightly arousal of longing; she promised her pain like a greater cosmos; but she felt that she, with her experienced sorrow, was still far behind the dark expectation that made this young girl beautiful.

Girls where I grew up. That the most beautiful among you might have found, on a summer afternoon in the darkened library, the small book printed by Jan des Tournes in 1556. That she might have taken the smooth, cooling volume out into the humming orchard or over to the phlox, in whose oversweet fragrance a sediment of sheer sweetness resides. That she might find the book early. In those days when her eyes are beginning to become aware while her mouth, younger, is still capable of biting off from an apple pieces that are much too large, and to be full.

And then girls when the time of more involving friendships comes, when it would be your secret to call to each other Dika and Anactoria, Gyrinno and Atthis. That someone, a neighbor perhaps, an older man, who had traveled in his youth and has long passed for an eccentric, betrays these names to you. That he sometimes invites you over for the sake of his famous peaches or the engravings of horseback riding in the white corridor upstairs, that were so much talked about that they had to be seen.

Perhaps you convince him to talk. Perhaps there is one among you who asks him to bring out his old travel diaries, who can tell? The same girl who one day manages to entice from him that isolated fragments of Sappho have come down to us, and who will not rest until she knows what was almost a secret: that this retiring man sometimes loved to turn his idleness to the translation of these fragments of poems. He has to admit that he has not thought of it for a long time, and what he has done, he assures her, is not worth mentioning. But still he is happy to recite a few strophes to these guile-less friends, if they strongly urge him to. He even discovers in his memory the Greek wording, he recites it because the translation, in his opinion, captures nothing, and to show these young people the beautiful, genuine fragment of the massive, ornate language that had been forged in such strong flames.

With all this he is again inspired to take up his work. There are lovely, almost youthful evenings for him, autumn evenings for ex-ample, that have much silent night before them. Then light burns long in his study. He does not always remain bent over the pages; he often leans back, closes his eyes over a line he has read again, and its sense diffuses into his blood. Never was he so convinced about antiquity. He might almost smile at the generations that mourned it like a lost play in which they would gladly have acted. Now in a flash he suddenly understands the vital significance of that early, unified world, which was something like a new, simultaneous infolding of all human endeavor. It does not deter him that that harmonious cul-ture with what was, in a sense, its complete unveiling of appearances, seemed to many later glances to form a whole, and a whole that was altogether past. To be sure, in that culture the divine half of life was really fitted to the semicircular bowl of existence the way two com-plete hemispheres come together to form a whole golden ball. But hardly had this happened when they, in their closed minds, felt this unstable realization only as a metaphor: the massive constellation itself lost substance and rose into space, mirroring in its golden cur-vature what was left behind, the sadness of what had not yet been mastered.

As he thinks this, the lonely man in his night, thinks and under-stands, he notices a plate with fruit on the windowsill. Spontaneously he selects an apple and places it in front of him on the table. How my life is around this fruit, he thought. Around everything complete rises what has not yet been done, growing in intensity.

And then there rises before him above the not yet done, almost too quickly, the small figure stretching out to infinity, whom (according to Galen's testimony) everyone was thinking of when they said: the poetess. For as the demolition and reconstruction of the world arose insistently behind the works of Heracles, so from the stocks of being in the deeds of her heart there surged forward to be lived the blessings and despairs with which time had to come to terms.

He suddenly knows this resolute heart that was ready to accomplish the whole of love up to the end. It did not surprise him that it had been misjudged; that one saw in these extremely future lovers only the excess, not the new measure of love and heart's sorrow. That one interpreted the inscription of their existence as happened to seem credible at the time, that one finally ascribed to her the death of those whom God encouraged singly to love out of themselves, without a response. Perhaps even among the friends she had formed there were some who did not grasp that at the height of their action they were lamenting not a person who left their embrace open, but lamenting the no longer possible that was worthy of their love.

Here the person reflecting stands up and goes over to his window. His high room is too close for him, he would like if possible to see the stars. He is not mistaken about himself. He knows that this emotion fills him because among the young girls of the neighborhood there is one who concerns him. He has desires (not for himself, no, but for her); for her he understands in a passing hour of the night the claim of love. He promises himself to say nothing of it to her. It seems to him most extreme to be alone and awake and to be thinking for her sake how very right that lover was: when she knew that union can mean nothing but an increase of loneliness; when she broke through the temporal goal of sex with what was its infinite purpose. When in the darkness of embraces she did not burrow for satiety, but for longing. When she despised the notion that of the two, one had to be the lover and one the beloved, and despised the weak beloved ones whom the lovers bore to bed for themselves, the beloved ones who then glowed within themselves into the lovers who abandoned them. From such high departures her heart became nature. She sang her bridesong about destiny to her mature favorites; extolled marriage to them; exaggerated for them the approaching husband, so that they would collect themselves for him as for a god and also surpass *his* glory.

Once, Abelone, in recent years, I felt you and understood you, unexpectedly, after not having thought about you for a long time.

It was in Venice, in autumn, in one of those salons in which foreigners gather for a while around the lady of the house, a foreigner herself. These people stand around with their cup of tea, and are charmed whenever an informed neighbor turns them quickly and discreetly toward the door to whisper a name that sounds Venetian. They are prepared for the most outlandish names, nothing can surprise them; for however meager their experience might be otherwise, in this city they nonchalantly entertain the most exaggerated possibilities. In their normal life they constantly confuse the exceptional with the forbidden, so that the expectation of the marvelous that they now permit themselves appears in their faces as a crude expression of excess. What happens to them at home for only a moment at concerts, or when they are alone with a novel, they make a show of here as a condition justified by these flattering surroundings. As, totally unprepared, aware of no danger, they let themselves be carried away by the almost fatal confessions of music as if by physical indiscretions, so they deliver themselves up to the gratifying swoon of gondolas without in the least coming to terms with the existence of Venice. No longer newly married couples, on their whole trip they have had only spiteful replies for each other, and sink to enduring one another in silence: the pleasant fatigue of his ideals comes over the man, while she feels herself young and nods encouragingly to the lethargic natives with a smile, as if she had teeth of sugar that were constantly dissolving. And if one listens, it turns out that they are leaving tomorrow or the day after or at the end of the week.

I stood there among them and was happy that I was not leaving. It will shortly turn cold. The soft, opiate Venice of their prejudices and needs disappears along with these somnolent foreigners, and one morning the *other* is here, real, alert, brittle to the point of shattering, not at all the dreamt-of city: Venice, willed forcibly out of nothing on sunken forests, and ultimately so *present* through and through. The hardened body, limited to what was most essential, through which the Arsenal,[24] waking through the night, drove the blood of its labor, and the mind and spirit of this body, more penetrating, continually expanding, which were stronger than the fragrance of aromatic lands. The suggestive State, which exchanged the salt and glass of its poverty for the treasures of peoples. The beautiful counterpoise to the world that even in its ornamentation contains energies whose nerves branch out ever more finely: this Venice.

The awareness that I knew this Venice came over me, in the

---

24   The shipyard of Venice.

midst of all these self-deceiving people, in so contradictory a fashion that I looked up in order to somehow express myself. Was it to be believed that there was not in these rooms a single person involuntarily waiting to be enlightened about the nature of these surroundings? A young person who would immediately understand that what was here exposed was not an easy enjoyment but an example of will, such as was nowhere else to be found more challenging or strict? I wandered around, my truth unsettled me. As it had taken hold of me here among so many people, it brought with it the desire to be uttered, defended, proven. The grotesque notion arose in me that the next moment I would clap my hands out of hatred against the misunderstanding that everyone was talking to death.

It was in this ridiculous mood that I noticed her. She was standing alone in front of a radiant window, observing me; not really with her eyes, which were serious and pensive, but actually with her mouth, which was ironically imitating the apparently angry expression of my face. I immediately felt the impatient tension in my features and assumed a composed expression, upon which her mouth became natural and arrogant. Then, after brief reflection, we simultaneously smiled at one another.

She was reminiscent, if you will, of a certain youthful portrait of the lovely Benedicte von Qualen who played a role in Baggesen's life. One could not see the dark silence of her eyes without suspecting the clear darkness of her voice. Moreover, the braiding of her hair and the neckline of her bright dress were so much Copenhagen that I resolved to speak to her in Danish.

But I wasn't close enough, and from the other side a current of people going toward her intervened; our Countess herself, delighted with her guests in her warm, enthusiastic distractedness, rushed up to her with a supporting crowd and led her off on the spot to sing.

I was convinced that the young girl would excuse herself by saying that no one in the company could be interested in hearing someone sing in Danish. As soon as she could get in a word, this is indeed what she said. The crowd around her bright figure became more pressing; someone knew that she could also sing in German. "And Italian," a laughing voice added with malicious conviction. I knew of no excuse that I could have wished for her, but I did not doubt that she would resist. Already a dry irritation was spreading across the faces of those urging her, weary from long smiling, already the good Countess, not to lose face, had sympathetically and with dignity re-treated a step; but then, when it was no longer at all necessary, the girl yielded. I felt myself grow pale with disappointment; my glance filled with reproach, but I turned away, there was no point in let-ting her see it. But she disengaged herself from the others and was suddenly at my side. Her dress shone at me, the flowery scent of her warmth enveloped me.

"I really am going to sing," she said along my cheek in Danish. "Not because they're asking, not to be polite: but because now I must sing."

The same malicious intolerance from which she had just liber-ated me poured forth from her words.

I slowly followed the group with which she moved away. But I stayed back at a tall door and let people move around and settle down. I leaned against the mirroring black door and waited. Some-one asked me what the preparations were for, whether someone was going to sing. I pretended not to know. While I lied she was already singing.

I couldn't see her. Gradually a space was created around one of those Italian songs that foreigners consider most genuine because their heritage is so obvious. She who was singing did not believe it.

She lifted it up with effort, she took it much too seriously. One recognized it was over by the applause from in front. I was sad and ashamed. There was some movement, and I thought that as soon as someone left I would leave too.

But then it suddenly became still. A stillness ensued that a moment before no one would have thought possible; it went on, it expanded, and now within it her voice rose. (Abelone, I thought. Abelone.) This time the voice was strong and full, but not heavy; of a piece, without a break, without a seam. It was an unknown German song. She sang it with remarkable simplicity, like something that imposed its own necessity. She sang:

"O woman whom I don't tell that at night I lie weeping,

you whose being makes me tired like a cradle.

You who do not tell me, when she wakens for me:

what if we were to bear this magnificence, without stilling, within us?

(short pause, then hesitantly)

Look at the lovers,

when first they begin to profess their love,

how soon they start lying."

Again stillness. God knows from whom it emanated. Then people stirred, bumped into one another, excused themselves, coughed. They were about to modulate into a general, blurring noise when suddenly the voice broke out, resolute, broad, and succinct:

"You alone make me. You alone I can transpose.

For a while it is you, then again it is the rustling,

or a fragrance that leaves no trace behind.

Alas, in your arms I have lost them all,

you alone, you are reborn again and again:

because I never held you I hold you fast."

No one had expected it. Everyone was standing as if humbled by this voice. And finally there was such a sureness in her, as if she had known for years that she would have had to step in at this moment.

Sometimes, earlier, I used to ask myself why Abelone did not apply the calories of her magnificent feeling to God. I know she longed to remove everything transitive from her love, but could her truthful heart deceive itself about God being only a direction of love, not an object of love? Didn't she know that no reciprocating love from Him need be feared? Didn't she know the restraint of this superior beloved, who calmly puts off desire in order to allow us slow ones to achieve our whole heart? Or did she want to avoid Christ? Was she afraid of being held up by him halfway on her journey, to become through him a beloved? Was that why she did not like to think of Julie Reventlow?

I almost think so when I reflect how such a naive lover as Mechthild, so ecstatic a lover as Teresa of Avila, so afflicted a lover as Blessed Rose of Lima, could sink down on this alleviation of God, yielding, but loved. Alas, the Christ who was a helper for the weak is wrong for these strong ones: where they no longer expected anything more than the infinite path, once more a formed being appears in the arching antechamber of heaven and spoils them with lodgings and confuses them with masculinity. The lens of his strongly breaking heart once more bends together the already parallel rays of their hearts, and they, whom the angels were hoping to preserve entirely for God, flame up in the aridity of their longing.

(To be loved means to burn up. Loving is: illuminating with inexhaustible oil. To be loved is to perish, loving is to endure.)[25]

---

25   Written in the margin of the manuscript (Rilke's note).

It is nonetheless possible that in later years Abelone did try to think with her heart in order to enter a relation with God directly and inconspicuously. I could imagine that there are letters from her reminiscent of the alert introspection of Princess Amalia Galitzin; but if these letters were addressed to someone to whom she had been close for years, how he might have suffered from the change in her. And she herself: I suspect she feared nothing but this spectral becoming different, which one doesn't notice because one constantly dismisses out of hand all the proofs of it as something most alien.

It will be hard to convince me that the story of the prodigal son is not the legend of him who did not want to be loved. When he was a child, everyone in the house loved him. He grew, he knew nothing different, and was at home in the softness of their hearts, as he was a child.

But as a boy he wanted to put aside what he was used to. He would not have been able to say it, but when he wandered around the countryside the whole day and did not even want the dogs along any more, it was because they loved him too; because observation and sympathy was in their glances, expectation and concern; and then too because one could not do anything in front of them without either pleasing or offending them. But what he was thinking at the time was really the inner indifference of his heart, which sometimes seized him early in the fields with such purity that he began to run so as not to have the time or breath to be more than an evanescent moment in which the morning awakens to consciousness.

The mystery of his life, a life that had never yet been, spread itself out before him. Spontaneously he left the footpath and ran further into the fields, his arms outstretched, as if in this openness he could master several distances at once. And then he threw himself down somewhere behind a hedge, and no one paid heed to him. He pared himself a flute, he threw a stone at a small beast of prey, he bent down and forced a beetle to turn around: all this was not a destiny, and the sky passed by as over nature. Finally the afternoon arrived with nothing but ideas: he was a buccaneer on the island of Tortuga, and there were no obligations connected with it; he laid siege to Campèche, he subdued Vera Cruz; he could be the whole army or a leader on horseback, or a ship on the sea: all according to what he felt like. But if it occurred to one to kneel, one was quickly Deodat von Gozon and had conquered the dragon and became aware, all hot as one was, that this heroism was haughtiness, without obedience. For one omitted nothing that was part of the experience. But however many fantasies suggested themselves, in between there was always time to be nothing but a bird, it was not clear what kind. Only that then it was time to go home.

My God, how much was there to be laid aside and forgotten; for it was necessary to really forget it; otherwise one betrays oneself when it surges up. However much one tarried and looked around, finally the gable came into view. The first window up there gazing at one, someone might well be standing there. The dogs, in whom expectation had been growing all day, came dashing through the bushes and drove one into being the person of their imagining. And the house did the rest. All one had to do was walk into its enveloping aroma, and it was already largely decided. Trifles might still change, but on the whole one was already the person they took one for; he for whom they had long since constructed a life out of his small past and their own desires, the being they had in common who stood day and night under the suggestiveness of their love, between their hopes and their suspicions, before their blame or applause.

For such a person it is no use climbing the steps with inexpressible caution. They will all be in the salon, and as soon as the door moves they look in that direction. He stays in the dark, he wants to wait for their questions. But then the worst happens. They take him by the hands, they draw him to the table, and everyone, as many as are there, lean forward with curiosity in front of the lamp. It's fine for them, they keep themselves dark, and on him falls, with the light, all the shame of having a face.

Will he stay and parrot the approximate life they ascribe to him, and with his whole countenance become like all of them? Will he divide himself between the tender truthfulness of his will and the blatant deceit that spoils them for him? Will he give up becoming what could only hurt those among his family whose weak heart is all that remains to them?

No, he will go away. For instance while they are all busy setting up for him the birthday table with the badly chosen objects meant to smooth things over yet once more. Go away for always. Only much later will it become clear to him how much he had planned at that time never to love, in order never to put anyone in the horrible situation of being loved. It occurs to him years later, and like other principles this one too has been impossible. For in his loneliness he had loved and loved again; each time squandering his entire nature and suffering incredible anxiety over the freedom of the other. He had slowly learned to suffuse the beloved object with the rays of his feeling, instead of consuming it in them. And he was spoiled by the delight of recognizing through the increasingly transparent form of the beloved those distances that opened up to his infinite desire for possession.

How he could then weep through whole nights with the longing to be suffused in that way himself. But a beloved who yields is still far from being a lover. O miserable nights in which he received his flooding gifts back again piecemeal, heavy with transience. How he then thought of the troubadours, who feared nothing more than having their longings heard. He would give all the money he had acquired and increased not to still have to experience that. He offended her with this crude payment, anxious from day to day that she might try to respond to his love. For he no longer hoped to experience the lover who would burst through him.

Even in the time when poverty terrified him daily with new deprivations, when his head was the favored plaything of misery and quite worn down, when sores opened everywhere on his body like fending eyes against the blackness of affliction, when he recoiled from the filth in which he had been abandoned because he was of his kind; still even then, when he thought about it, his greatest horror was of being responded to. What were all the darknesses since against the intense sadness of those embraces in which everything was lost. Did not one wake up with the feeling of being without a future? Did one not go around mindlessly without the right to any danger? Had one not had to promise a hundred times not to die? Perhaps it was the stubbornness of this unpleasant memory that from recurrence to recurrence tried to maintain a place that would allow his life among the castoffs to endure. Finally he was found again. And only then, only in his years as a shepherd, did all that constituted the many parts of his past die down.

Who can describe what was happening to him then? What poet has the persuasiveness to reconcile the length of those days with the shortness of life? What art is broad enough to evoke at the same time his slender, cloaked figure and the whole enveloping space of his gigantic nights?

That was the time that began with his feeling dispersed and anonymous, like one who is haltingly recuperating. He did not love, unless he loved to be. The low love of his sheep did not concern him; his love scattered itself about him and shimmered gently over the meadows like light falling through clouds. Following the guiltless trace of its hunger, he strode silent across the meadows of the world. Strangers saw him on the Acropolis, and perhaps he was for a long time one of the shepherds in Les Baux and saw enstoned time survive the high race that, in spite of its achievement of seven and three, was never able to conquer the sixteen rays of its star. Or should I imagine him in Orange, resting in the triumphal gate in the countryside? Or see him in the Alyscamps that was accustomed to shades, his glance following a dragonfly among the graves, which stand open like the graves of the resurrected?

No matter. I see more than him, I see his existence, which at that time was beginning the long love to God, the silent, goal-less task. For once again the growing inability of his heart to do otherwise came over him, who had wanted to hold himself back for always. And this time he hoped to be heard. His entire being, which through his long solitude had become sensitive and unwavering, promised that He of whom he was now thinking understood how to love with a penetrating, radiant love. But while he longed finally to be loved so masterfully, his feeling, accustomed to distances, understood how extremely far away God was. Nights came in which he thought he would throw himself upon Him into space; hours full of discovery in which he felt strong enough to dive into the earth in order to seize it and bear it up on the stormflood of his heart. He was like one who hears a glorious language and feverishly undertakes to write poetry in it. Still ahead was the consternation of discovering how difficult this language was; at first he did not want to believe that a long life could be spent forming the first, short, false sentences that are without meaning. He plunged into learning it like a runner into a race, but the density of what he had to master slowed him down. Nothing was more humbling than this being at the beginning. He had found the wise man's stone, and now he was incessantly being forced to transform the quickly made gold of his happiness into the lead clumps of patience. He, who had adapted himself to space, now burrowed like a worm, winding passages without exit or direction. Now that he was learning to love, sorrowfully and with so much effort, it was shown to him how careless and insignificant all the previous love he thought he had accomplished had been. How nothing could have come from any of that love because he had not begun to work at it and turn it into reality.

In those years great changes took place in him. He nearly forgot God through the hard work of approaching Him, and all that he perhaps hoped to achieve in time by reaching Him was "sa patience de supporter une âme."[26] The accidents of fate that people hold to had long fallen away from him and had now lost even their spiced, bitter taste that was needed for pleasure and pain, and had become for him pure and nourishing. From the roots of his being there developed the firm, overwintering plant of a fruitful joyousness. He was totally immersed in gaining mastery of his inner life; he did not want to overlook anything, for he did not doubt that his love was in all of it, and increasing. Indeed his inner resolve went so far that he was determined to make up for the most important things he had earlier not been able to accomplish, that he had simply waited through. He

---

26 "his patience to endure a soul."

thought above all of his childhood, and the more calmly he thought about it the more it seemed to him unfinished. All his memories of it had the vagueness of intimations about them, and that they were deemed past made them almost future. To take all this upon himself once more, and now truly, was the reason the estranged one returned home. We do not know whether he stayed; we know only that he came back.

Those who have told the story try at this point to remind us of the house as it was; for there only a little time has passed, a little counted time, everyone in the house can tell how much. The dogs have grown old, but they are still alive. It is reported that one of them started howling. An interruption goes through the whole work of the day. Faces appear in the windows, aged and grownup faces of moving likeness. And in one quite old countenance suddenly recognition bursts through, pale. Recognition? Really only recognition?— Forgiveness. Forgiveness of what?—Love. My God: love.

He who had been recognized had no longer thought of that, preoccupied as he was: that there could still be love. It is understandable that of all that now took place only this has been handed down: his gesture, the incredible gesture that had never before been seen; the gesture of pleading with which he threw himself at their feet, begging them not to love. Frightened and unsteady, they raised him up to themselves. They interpreted his impetuosity in their fashion by forgiving him. It must have been indescribably liberating for him that they all misunderstood him, in spite of the desperate unambiguity of his posture. Apparently he could stay. For he recognized more from day to day that the love they were so vain about and secretly encouraged each other to had nothing to do with him. He almost had to smile when they made such efforts, and it was clear how little the others could be meaning him.

What did they know who he was. He was now terribly difficult to love, and he felt that only One was capable of it. But He did not yet want to.

End of the Notebooks

A Note on Rilke's Sources

Rilke's sources were numerous and often obscure. Simply identifying this or that historical figure, as the notes to previous translations have done, does not give an indication of the astonishing sweep of sources he consulted or his reasons for weaving so many disparate and unacknowledged threads into the complex fabric of his novel. Rilke was obsessed with accuracy to reality. In working on his only novel, he pursued, in addition to his considerable knowledge of art, extraordinarily detailed antiquarian research into German, French, Danish, Swedish, and Russian historical sources, which he incorporated and adapted to reflect Malte. He never simply copies the accounts from his sources, but weaves them into his artistic purpose.

The depth of Rilke's use of research for and in this novel is astonishing. A partial listing of the sources he employed in some form includes: *Frau Maria Grubbe* and *Niels Lyhne*, novellas by the Danish writer Jens Peter Jakobsen; *Efterlade Papirer fra den Reventlowske Familiekreds i Tidsrummet 1770–1827*; *Johann Caspar Lavaters Rejse til Danmark i Sommeren 1793*; *Danske Malede Portraeter*; articles from the *Allgemeine Encyclopädie der Wissenschaften und Künste*, edited by Ersch and Gruber; Baluzius's *Vitae paparum avenionesium*; Barante's *Histoire des ducs de Bourgogne de la maison de Valois,*

1364–1477; the anonymous *Chronique du religieux de Saint-Denys, contenant le règne de Charles VI, de 1380 à 1422*; Jean de Juvénal des Ursins, *Histoire de Charles VI, roy de France . . . depuis 1380 jusqu'à 1422*; Pushkin's *Boris Gudunov* and possibly the Russian historians Karamsin and Soloviov. The list goes on, and not all Rilke's sources have been identified. In composing Malte's accounts he frequently combined a number of them.

One of Rilke's sources for Malte's re-inscribing of medieval stories was the *Chronicles* of Jean Froissart (c. 1338–c.1410), to which he was apparently introduced by the sculptor Rodin. These are accounts from a time when, as Rilke wrote in his *Requiem* for Count Kalckreuth, "happening was still visible." (Walter Scott wrote of Froissart: "Whoever has not taken up the chronicle of Froissart must have been dull indeed if he did not find himself transported back to the days of Cressy and Poictiers. In truth, his history has less the air of a narrative than of a dramatic representation. The figures live and move before us; we not only know what they did, but learn the mode and process of the action, and the very words with which it was accompanied. This sort of colloquial history is of all others the most interesting.")

Malte's retelling of these old tales, names, and figures is vivid, but baffling to the modern reader. They would also have baffled the novel's first readers, who would at least have recognized Ibsen, Beethoven, Duse, and the tapestries of The Lady with the Unicorn, as well as some of the places in Paris and France and some of the literary references. But who were Charles the Sixth, Grischka Otrepioff the false Demetrius, Gaspara Stampa, and the early nineteenth-century Danish poets Jens Baggesen and Adam Öhlenschläger? What were, for example, "the horns of Uri" that betokened the defeat of Charles the Bold in the battle of Nancy in 1477? (They were alpenhorn signals transmitted over great distances by Swiss peasants, employed in the battle.) What reader can follow Malte's (accurate) description of the different kinds of lace? Like his Felix Arvers (a real Danish poet), Rilke "was a poet, and hated the approximate." All the obscure figures, names, and events Malte conjures up are historically documented. They were real in their own time, and have survived through their works, portraits, and historical accounts. This is largely true as well of the incidents of Malte's Scandinavian childhood. He seeks to make all these now invisible pasts visible once more by re-inscribing their stories through the lens of his own seeing. Dedicated as he was to the reality of his sources, however, Rilke was serious when he said in the letter to his Polish translator quoted in the Introduction that these figures are to be understood not as historical references but as "*words of [Malte's] desperate need*" (his emphasis). Making the real past live again is not to be understood for its own sake, but as Malte's attempt to shore up his own faltering but dogged quest to be an artist.

Rilke's elaborate use of sources exemplifies, in one way or another, Malte's intense desire to create art in the present (including the present of the reader reading the *Notebooks*) out of long-forgotten real life, and also to champion a kind of love of which he feels himself incapable. The same impulse informs Malte's spooky walk through the portrait gallery at Ulsgaard as he brings to life the portraits and loves of ancestral lords and ladies, or when he wraps himself up in old costumes and masks he finds hanging forgotten in attic closets, in both cases hauntingly and beautifully re-animating past presences in his and the reader's present time. (A comparison with Rilke's similar use of obscure references in the *Duino Elegies* would be instructive.) All these obscurities of the past are to be understood as raw material stored in Malte's mind for possible transmutation into poetry, but he can not transform their potential. Rilke the writer, however, does and can: each episode is beautifully formed as a kind of prose poem. There is a constant undercurrent, made explicit in the closing pages in the account of the Prodigal Son, that Malte can not achieve his breakthrough in art until he learns to love; and this task Rilke leaves open.

Here are several samples of Rilke's use of source material. You will notice that the historical information in itself does not help in understanding the novel; the reader is constantly thrown back on Malte's own emotion in revivifying it.

Christian IV, 1577–1648, King of Denmark. Rilke took the account of the king's death from *Danske Malede Portraeter*, and left the king's final outburst ("døden, døden") in Danish in the *Notebooks*.

Bettina von Arnim, 1785–1859, published *Goethe's Correspondence with a Child* in 1835. At age 22, in 1807, Bettina had been introduced through his mother to Goethe, who was almost 60. The meeting, which may have been somewhat flirtatious, led to the subsequent correspondence. Bettina later embroidered it quite a bit for publication. Malte, taking the exchange at face value, clearly favors the youthful ardor of her letters over Goethe's guarded responses, for Rilke a demonstration of the superior power of woman's power to love over man's.

Gaspara Stampa, c. 1523–1554, wrote poems about her great abiding love for Count Collatino de Collato, who did not fully reciprocate her passion. For Malte she exemplified the power of woman's love that transcends its male object.

Ivan Grosny, Czar Ivan IV The Terrible, 1530–1584, a cruel, sadistic tyrant. In 1584 his heir, the czarevich Dmitri (Demetrius),

1582–1591, was displaced as Czar (he was two when his father died) by his brother Feodor I, but the real ruler of Russia during Feodor's reign was Boris Godunov, who may have had Dmitri killed. Four pretenders claiming to be Dmitri subsequently appeared; the first (the one Rilke identifies as Grishka Otrepioff) showed up in Poland and invaded Russia in 1604. When Boris died in 1605, this false Dmitri was crowned Czar. For marrying a Polish noblewoman, Marina Mniszech, he was hated by the Russian boyars, who killed him in an uprising in 1606. The leader of the boyars, Prince Vasily Shuiski, became Czar Vasily IV. In 1607 another false Dmitri appeared, and Marina identified him as her husband. This pretender was killed in 1610. (Two later false Dmitris were executed.) Malte invests the players in this tangled tale with a vibrant intensity that reflects his own intense emotional feeling as he seeks to revivify a tempestuous past when happening was visible.

Marianna Alcoforado, the Portuguese nun, 1640–1723, whose letters to her lover, the Marquis de Chamilly, are famous for their frankness, eloquence, and passion. To avoid scandal Chamilly, a French army officer, returned to France. For Malte this is another example of woman's love surpassing man's.

Charles the Bold, 1433–1477, Duke of Burgundy from 1476, who was defeated and killed in the battle of Nancy in 1477, and whose frozen corpse was discovered by the duke's page and a poor laundress of his household.

Jean de Cahors (Pope John XXII), 1245–1334. pope 1316–1334, reigned at Avignon. He became embroiled in a bitter quarrel with Ludwig IV of Bavaria after Ludwig became Holy Roman Emperor; the pope claimed authority over the Empire. Ludwig invaded Italy and briefly established an antipope, which undercut the papal claims.

In his late years, John advocated a theory of the vision of God that was ridiculed by theologians, and he subsequently retracted it. For Malte he represents a world order that revolved around the powerful passions of formidable public figures who were able to make happening visible, even in a world torn apart by dissensions.

P X. - Valéry - pure retina
XII, for the sake of a single verse

SELECTED DALKEY ARCHIVE PAPERBACKS

PETROS ABATZOGLOU, *What Does Mrs. Freeman Want?*
PIERRE ALBERT-BIROT, *Grabinoulor.*
YUZ ALESHKOVSKY, *Kangaroo.*
FELIPE ALFAU, *Chromos.*
    Locos.
IVAN ÂNGELO, *The Celebration.*
    The Tower of Glass.
DAVID ANTIN, *Talking.*
ANTÓNIO LOBO ANTUNES, *Knowledge of Hell.*
ALAIN ARIAS-MISSON, *Theatre of Incest.*
JOHN ASHBERY AND JAMES SCHUYLER, *A Nest of Ninnies.*
DJUNA BARNES, *Ladies Almanack.*
    Ryder.
JOHN BARTH, *LETTERS.*
    Sabbatical.
DONALD BARTHELME, *The King.*
    Paradise.
SVETISLAV BASARA, *Chinese Letter.*
MARK BINELLI, *Sacco and Vanzetti Must Die!*
ANDREI BITOV, *Pushkin House.*
LOUIS PAUL BOON, *Chapel Road.*
    Summer in Termuren.
ROGER BOYLAN, *Killoyle.*
IGNÁCIO DE LOYOLA BRANDÃO, *Teeth under the Sun.*
    Zero.
BONNIE BREMSER, *Troia: Mexican Memoirs.*
CHRISTINE BROOKE-ROSE, *Amalgamemnon.*
BRIGID BROPHY, *In Transit.*
MEREDITH BROSNAN, *Mr. Dynamite.*
GERALD L. BRUNS,
    Modern Poetry and the Idea of Language.
EVGENY BUNIMOVICH AND J. KATES, EDS.,
    Contemporary Russian Poetry: An Anthology.
GABRIELLE BURTON, *Heartbreak Hotel.*
MICHEL BUTOR, *Degrees.*
    Mobile.
    Portrait of the Artist as a Young Ape.
G. CABRERA INFANTE, *Infante's Inferno.*
    Three Trapped Tigers.
JULIETA CAMPOS, *The Fear of Losing Eurydice.*
ANNE CARSON, *Eros the Bittersweet.*
CAMILO JOSÉ CELA, *Christ versus Arizona.*
    The Family of Pascual Duarte.
    The Hive.
LOUIS-FERDINAND CÉLINE, *Castle to Castle.*
    Conversations with Professor Y.
    London Bridge.
    North.
    Rigadoon.
HUGO CHARTERIS, *The Tide Is Right.*
JEROME CHARYN, *The Tar Baby.*
MARC CHOLODENKO, *Mordechai Schamz.*
EMILY HOLMES COLEMAN, *The Shutter of Snow.*
ROBERT COOVER, *A Night at the Movies.*
STANLEY CRAWFORD, *Log of the S.S. The Mrs Unguentine.*
    Some Instructions to My Wife.
ROBERT CREELEY, *Collected Prose.*
RENÉ CREVEL, *Putting My Foot in It.*
RALPH CUSACK, *Cadenza.*
SUSAN DAITCH, *L.C.*
    Storytown.
NICHOLAS DELBANCO, *The Count of Concord.*
NIGEL DENNIS, *Cards of Identity.*
PETER DIMOCK,
    A Short Rhetoric for Leaving the Family.
ARIEL DORFMAN, *Konfidenz.*
COLEMAN DOWELL, *The Houses of Children.*
    Island People.
    Too Much Flesh and Jabez.
ARKADII DRAGOMOSHCHENKO, *Dust.*
RIKKI DUCORNET, *The Complete Butcher's Tales.*
    The Fountains of Neptune.
    The Jade Cabinet.
    The One Marvelous Thing.
    Phosphor in Dreamland.
    The Stain.
    The Word "Desire."
WILLIAM EASTLAKE, *The Bamboo Bed.*
    Castle Keep.
    Lyric of the Circle Heart.
JEAN ECHENOZ, *Chopin's Move.*
STANLEY ELKIN, *A Bad Man.*
    Boswell: A Modern Comedy.
    Criers and Kibitzers, Kibitzers and Criers.
    The Dick Gibson Show.
    The Franchiser.
    George Mills.
    The Living End.
    The MacGuffin.
    The Magic Kingdom.
    Mrs. Ted Bliss.
    The Rabbi of Lud.
    Van Gogh's Room at Arles.
ANNIE ERNAUX, *Cleaned Out.*

LAUREN FAIRBANKS, *Muzzle Thyself.*
    Sister Carrie.
LESLIE A. FIEDLER, *Love and Death in the American Novel.*
GUSTAVE FLAUBERT, *Bouvard and Pécuchet.*
KASS FLEISHER, *Talking out of School.*
FORD MADOX FORD, *The March of Literature.*
JON FOSSE, *Melancholy.*
MAX FRISCH, *I'm Not Stiller.*
    Man in the Holocene.
CARLOS FUENTES, *Christopher Unborn.*
    Distant Relations.
    Terra Nostra.
    Where the Air Is Clear.
JANICE GALLOWAY, *Foreign Parts.*
    The Trick Is to Keep Breathing.
WILLIAM H. GASS, *Cartesian Sonata and Other Novellas.*
    A Temple of Texts.
    The Tunnel.
    Willie Masters' Lonesome Wife.
ETIENNE GILSON, *The Arts of the Beautiful.*
    Forms and Substances in the Arts.
C. S. GISCOMBE, *Giscome Road.*
    Here.
    Prairie Style.
DOUGLAS GLOVER, *Bad News of the Heart.*
    The Enamoured Knight.
WITOLD GOMBROWICZ, *A Kind of Testament.*
KAREN ELIZABETH GORDON, *The Red Shoes.*
GEORGI GOSPODINOV, *Natural Novel.*
JUAN GOYTISOLO, *Count Julian.*
    Makbara.
    Marks of Identity.
PATRICK GRAINVILLE, *The Cave of Heaven.*
HENRY GREEN, *Blindness.*
    Concluding.
    Doting.
    Nothing.
JIŘÍ GRUŠA, *The Questionnaire.*
GABRIEL GUDDING, *Rhode Island Notebook.*
JOHN HAWKES, *Whistlejacket.*
AIDAN HIGGINS, *A Bestiary.*
    Bornholm Night-Ferry.
    Flotsam and Jetsam.
    Langrishe, Go Down.
    Scenes from a Receding Past.
    Windy Arbours.
ALDOUS HUXLEY, *Antic Hay.*
    Crome Yellow.
    Point Counter Point.
    Those Barren Leaves.
    Time Must Have a Stop.
MIKHAIL IOSSEL AND JEFF PARKER, EDS., *Amerika:*
    Contemporary Russians View the United States.
GERT JONKE, *Geometric Regional Novel.*
    Homage to Czerny.
JACQUES JOUET, *Mountain R.*
HUGH KENNER, *The Counterfeiters.*
    Flaubert, Joyce and Beckett: The Stoic Comedians.
    Joyce's Voices.
DANILO KIŠ, *Garden, Ashes.*
    A Tomb for Boris Davidovich.
ANITA KONKKA, *A Fool's Paradise.*
GEORGE KONRÁD, *The City Builder.*
TADEUSZ KONWICKI, *A Minor Apocalypse.*
    The Polish Complex.
MENIS KOUMANDAREAS, *Koula.*
ELAINE KRAF, *The Princess of 72nd Street.*
JIM KRUSOE, *Iceland.*
EWA KURYLUK, *Century 21.*
ERIC LAURRENT, *Do Not Touch.*
VIOLETTE LEDUC, *La Bâtarde.*
DEBORAH LEVY, *Billy and Girl.*
    Pillow Talk in Europe and Other Places.
JOSÉ LEZAMA LIMA, *Paradiso.*
ROSA LIKSOM, *Dark Paradise.*
OSMAN LINS, *Avalovara.*
    The Queen of the Prisons of Greece.
ALF MAC LOCHLAINN, *The Corpus in the Library.*
    Out of Focus.
RON LOEWINSOHN, *Magnetic Field(s).*
BRIAN LYNCH, *The Winner of Sorrow.*
D. KEITH MANO, *Take Five.*
MICHELINE AHARONIAN MARCOM, *The Mirror in the Well.*
BEN MARCUS, *The Age of Wire and String.*
WALLACE MARKFIELD, *Teitlebaum's Window.*
    To an Early Grave.
DAVID MARKSON, *Reader's Block.*
    Springer's Progress.
    Wittgenstein's Mistress.
CAROLE MASO, *AVA.*
LADISLAV MATEJKA AND KRYSTYNA POMORSKA, EDS.,
    Readings in Russian Poetics: Formalist and
    Structuralist Views.

www.dalkeyarchive.com

SELECTED DALKEY ARCHIVE PAPERBACKS

HARRY MATHEWS,
  The Case of the Persevering Maltese: Collected Essays.
  Cigarettes.
  The Conversions.
  The Human Country: New and Collected Stories.
  The Journalist.
  My Life in CIA.
  Singular Pleasures.
  The Sinking of the Odradek Stadium.
  Tlooth.
  20 Lines a Day.
ROBERT L. MCLAUGHLIN, ED.,
  Innovations: An Anthology of Modern &
    Contemporary Fiction.
HERMAN MELVILLE, *The Confidence-Man.*
AMANDA MICHALOPOULOU, *I'd Like.*
STEVEN MILLHAUSER, *The Barnum Museum.*
  In the Penny Arcade.
RALPH J. MILLS, JR., *Essays on Poetry.*
OLIVE MOORE, *Spleen.*
NICHOLAS MOSLEY, *Accident.*
  Assassins.
  Catastrophe Practice.
  Children of Darkness and Light.
  Experience and Religion.
  The Hesperides Tree.
  Hopeful Monsters.
  Imago Bird.
  Impossible Object.
  Inventing God.
  Judith.
  Look at the Dark.
  Natalie Natalia.
  Serpent.
  Time at War.
  The Uses of Slime Mould: Essays of Four Decades.
WARREN F. MOTTE, JR.,
  Fables of the Novel: French Fiction since 1990.
  Fiction Now: The French Novel in the 21st Century.
  Oulipo: A Primer of Potential Literature.
YVES NAVARRE, *Our Share of Time.*
  Sweet Tooth.
DOROTHY NELSON, *In Night's City.*
  Tar and Feathers.
WILFRIDO D. NOLLEDO, *But for the Lovers.*
FLANN O'BRIEN, *At Swim-Two-Birds.*
  At War.
  The Best of Myles.
  The Dalkey Archive.
  Further Cuttings.
  The Hard Life.
  The Poor Mouth.
  The Third Policeman.
CLAUDE OLLIER, *The Mise-en-Scène.*
PATRIK OUŘEDNÍK, *Europeana.*
FERNANDO DEL PASO, *Palinuro of Mexico.*
ROBERT PINGET, *The Inquisitory.*
  Mahu or The Material.
  Trio.
RAYMOND QUENEAU, *The Last Days.*
  Odile.
  Pierrot Mon Ami.
  Saint Glinglin.
ANN QUIN, *Berg.*
  Passages.
  Three.
  Tripticks.
ISHMAEL REED, *The Free-Lance Pallbearers.*
  The Last Days of Louisiana Red.
  Reckless Eyeballing.
  The Terrible Threes.
  The Terrible Twos.
  Yellow Back Radio Broke-Down.
JEAN RICARDOU, *Place Names.*
RAINER MARIA RILKE,
  The Notebooks of Malte Laurids Brigge.
JULIÁN RÍOS, *Larva: A Midsummer Night's Babel.*
  Poundemonium.
AUGUSTO ROA BASTOS, *I the Supreme.*
OLIVIER ROLIN, *Hotel Crystal.*
JACQUES ROUBAUD, *The Great Fire of London.*
  Hortense in Exile.
  Hortense Is Abducted.
  The Plurality of Worlds of Lewis.
  The Princess Hoppy.
  The Form of a City Changes Faster, Alas,
    Than the Human Heart.
  Some Thing Black.
LEON S. ROUDIEZ, *French Fiction Revisited.*

VEDRANA RUDAN, *Night.*
LYDIE SALVAYRE, *The Company of Ghosts.*
  Everyday Life.
  The Lecture.
  The Power of Flies.
LUIS RAFAEL SÁNCHEZ, *Macho Camacho's Beat.*
SEVERO SARDUY, *Cobra & Maitreya.*
NATHALIE SARRAUTE, *Do You Hear Them?*
  Martereau.
  The Planetarium.
ARNO SCHMIDT, *Collected Stories.*
  Nobodaddy's Children.
CHRISTINE SCHUTT, *Nightwork.*
GAIL SCOTT, *My Paris.*
JUNE AKERS SEESE,
  Is This What Other Women Feel Too?
  What Waiting Really Means.
AURELIE SHEEHAN, *Jack Kerouac Is Pregnant.*
VIKTOR SHKLOVSKY, *Knight's Move.*
  A Sentimental Journey: Memoirs 1917–1922.
  Energy of Delusion: A Book on Plot.
  Literature and Cinematography.
  Theory of Prose.
  Third Factory.
  Zoo, or Letters Not about Love.
JOSEF ŠKVORECKÝ,
  The Engineer of Human Souls.
CLAUDE SIMON, *The Invitation.*
GILBERT SORRENTINO, *Aberration of Starlight.*
  Blue Pastoral.
  Crystal Vision.
  Imaginative Qualities of Actual Things.
  Mulligan Stew.
  Pack of Lies.
  Red the Fiend.
  The Sky Changes.
  Something Said.
  Splendide-Hôtel.
  Steelwork.
  Under the Shadow.
W. M. SPACKMAN, *The Complete Fiction.*
GERTRUDE STEIN, *Lucy Church Amiably.*
  The Making of Americans.
  A Novel of Thank You.
PIOTR SZEWC, *Annihilation.*
STEFAN THEMERSON, *Hobson's Island.*
  The Mystery of the Sardine.
  Tom Harris.
JEAN-PHILIPPE TOUSSAINT, *The Bathroom.*
  Camera.
  Monsieur.
  Television.
DUMITRU TSEPENEAG, *Pigeon Post.*
  Vain Art of the Fugue.
ESTHER TUSQUETS, *Stranded.*
DUBRAVKA UGRESIC, *Lend Me Your Character.*
  Thank You for Not Reading.
MATI UNT, *Diary of a Blood Donor.*
  Things in the Night.
ÁLVARO URIBE AND OLIVIA SEARS, EDS.,
  The Best of Contemporary Mexican Fiction.
ELOY URROZ, *The Obstacles.*
LUISA VALENZUELA, *He Who Searches.*
PAUL VERHAEGHEN, *Omega Minor.*
MARJA-LIISA VARTIO, *The Parson's Widow.*
BORIS VIAN, *Heartsnatcher.*
AUSTRYN WAINHOUSE, *Hedyphagetica.*
PAUL WEST, *Words for a Deaf Daughter & Gala.*
CURTIS WHITE, *America's Magic Mountain.*
  The Idea of Home.
  Memories of My Father Watching TV.
  Monstrous Possibility: An Invitation to
    Literary Politics.
  Requiem.
DIANE WILLIAMS, *Excitability: Selected Stories.*
  Romancer Erector.
DOUGLAS WOOLF, *Wall to Wall.*
  Ya! & John-Juan.
JAY WRIGHT, *Polynomials and Pollen.*
  The Presentable Art of Reading Absence.
PHILIP WYLIE, *Generation of Vipers.*
MARGUERITE YOUNG, *Angel in the Forest.*
  Miss MacIntosh, My Darling.
REYOUNG, *Unbabbling.*
ZORAN ŽIVKOVIĆ, *Hidden Camera.*
LOUIS ZUKOFSKY, *Collected Fiction.*
SCOTT ZWIREN, *God Head.*

FOR A FULL LIST OF PUBLICATIONS, VISIT:
www.dalkeyarchive.com